Y0-BXC-938

# Tim Pelham's "Ideal Mate" Worksheet:

**MUST HAVE**
Pleasant voice (Nothing too high-pitched or screechy)
Sense of humor (Or at least she should *pretend* to get my jokes)
Sex appeal (My biggest turn-on is a woman with curves and confidence)

**WILL SETTLE FOR**
A woman who isn't a sports fanatic (Provided she doesn't mind if *I* am!)
A woman who already turned me down once before, in favor of Mr. Wrong (As long as she doesn't make that mistake again)

***DEAL BREAKER***
*The woman must make me forget my acute commitment phobia. In short, she has to be Sarah Dann...!*

*Dear Reader,*

Being single has a lot of compensations. No one bothers you to clean the clutter off the coffee table. If you feel like having cereal or—better yet!—microwave popcorn for dinner, no one bugs you about cooking a "real" meal. And there's plenty of room on the couch for you and all three cats. But sometimes dating is fun, too. You know…dinners out. *Real* dinners. Snuggling on the couch—cats optional—while watching a video and eating that microwave popcorn. But where do you go to find Mr. Let's-Go-Out? How about a class? That's right, a class like "Dating for Destiny," as taught by Sarah Dann, heroine of Diane Pershing's *Third Date's the Charm.* Romance finds Sarah, that's for sure. So where do I sign up?

Then there's our second book this month, Marie Ferrarella's *Mommy and the Policeman Next Door.* This story may feature the world's first crayoned ransom note. Of course, what would you expect when eight-year-old twins decide the perfect man for Mom is the cop next door? How better to introduce them than by a nice—fake!—kidnapping? Luckily he's been wanting an introduction to the lady for a while, so he's more than happy to take the Case of the Not-Exactly-Missing Mom.

Enjoy! And come back next month for two more terrific books about unexpectedly meeting, dating—and marrying!—Mr. Right.

Leslie Wainger
**Senior Editor and Editorial Coordinator**

Please address questions and book requests to:
Silhouette Reader Service
U.S.: 3010 Walden Ave., P.O. Box 1325, Buffalo, NY 14269
Canadian: P.O. Box 609, Fort Erie, Ont. L2A 5X3

# DIANE PERSHING

## Third Date's the Charm

Published by Silhouette Books
America's Publisher of Contemporary Romance

Heartfelt thanks:
To Carol Kirschner, for inspiration
To Toby Berlin, for background
To Jodie George, for guidance

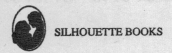 SILHOUETTE BOOKS

ISBN 0-373-52050-6

THIRD DATE'S THE CHARM

## *About the author*

### DIANE PERSHING

I cannot remember a time when I didn't have my nose buried in a book. As a child I would cheat the bedtime curfew by snuggling under the covers with my teddy bear, a flashlight and a forbidden (read "grown-up") novel. My mom warned me that I would ruin my eyes, but so far, they still work.

*Third Date's the Charm* was inspired by a friend who teaches a class similar to Dating For Destiny, and through the class she actually did meet the man she eventually married. Isn't it nice to know there are still miracles?

I live in Los Angeles, and am only slightly affected, I promise. My life is a fine one. My two children, Morgan Rose and Ben, are both in college, and I enjoy a fun career as a voice-over performer. I even get to have this second career, as a writer of romances. How lucky can a person get?

**Books by Diane Pershing**

**Silhouette Yours Truly**

*First Date: Honeymoon*
*Third Date's the Charm*

## 1

**K**eep On Learning!

Tim barely noted the name engraved on the side of the small stone building as he bounded up the stairs, two at a time. Pushing open the double doors, he rubbed his hand over his chin and winced. Major bristles. Probably should have shaved before meeting Gail, but he'd rushed over directly from the newsroom and a late-breaking story. Maybe the two of them could make it a short evening so he could get back to work.

Walking briskly past two large potted plants, he hurried along a corridor with fluorescent-lit ceilings and walls covered with bulletin boards. Your basic school, Tim thought, adult-education variety. Except for the pink-, salmon- and orange-colored walls. And except for some of the notices: large posters promoted the usual Desktop Publishing and Tips on Becoming a Travel Agent. There was also Mushroom Farming For Profit and How To Be a Successful Dominatrix.

Oh, yeah? Tim grinned. Not quite a typical school, after all.

Gail had told him to meet her outside room 12, and there it was. The door was bright orange, in keeping with the general color scheme the whole school seemed to be splashed with. Whoever had designed the decor had definitely been in a merry mood.

A table was set up outside the classroom, behind which sat a plump middle-aged lady with rimless glasses, chatting with people as she checked off names on a piece of paper. Tim ambled up to her. "Excuse me. I'm supposed to be meeting someone here. Gail Conklin?"

The lady perused her list, then shook her head. "No Gail Conklin here. Are you signed up for this class, Mr.—?"

"Pelham. Tim Pelham. And I don't know anything about a class. I'm just supposed to show up, I guess."

"I'm Liz, by the way." She pointed to the bright yellow name tag on her shoulder as she scanned the page again. "Sorry. No Conklin. But there *is* a Pelham. Yes, here you are. Oh, and here's a note someone left for you."

Smiling cheerfully, she handed him an envelope with renderings of vines and flowers squiggled all over it. He thanked her and tore the flap open, wondering what Gail was up to this time.

Dear Tim,
In case you can't tell, I'm not here. In fact, I'm not in San Francisco at all. A few days ago, Darrel, my old boyfriend, came back to town. He's been traveling all around the country on his motorcycle having adventures and he invited me to go along. It sounded so right, you know? So I'm off to explore my destiny. You know me—spur-of-the-moment Gail. Ha-ha.

But seriously, I'm really sorry. I hope you don't mind too much. I had signed up for this class because you and I talked about how there's always been something missing between us, and I figured, why not give this a try? Then Darrel showed up. So now I'm giving the class to you as a gift—yes, I paid for it, did you ever think you'd see the day? Ha-ha. You never know, you might meet someone to replace me *right away!* Good luck.

Love, Gail.

Motorcycle? Class? Tim scratched his head. What was going on?

"Here's your course material, Mr. Pelham," Liz said. "The others are inside already."

Thoroughly confused, Tim glanced at the small orange booklet she'd handed him, then read the words in bold royal blue letters on the front.

## Dating For Destiny
### *A Sure-Fire Way To Meet That Special Someone*

Raising his head, Tim peered through the open door of classroom 12. A whole bunch of men and women sat in chairs and fidgeted, their eyes darting from one person to the next to the next. No one was talking to anyone else, but you could practically taste the air of nervous excitement. There was more than one decent-looking woman in there, he noted absently as he scanned the room, and a couple of them caught him staring at them and stared right back.

Averting his gaze, he glanced again at the booklet.

Dating For Destiny?

All of a sudden, Gail's rejection registered. Tim had been dumped.

Dumped!

But...how could she?

Not that he'd been in love with Gail, or she with him. Not that they'd made any future plans, but they had enjoyed each other's company. Hadn't they? Well...at first, anyway.

And they had *talked about* talking about living together. Although that had been a while ago. And it had been a really brief discussion, on both their parts; they'd picked it up and set it down like a foreign, potentially troublesome spice you weren't sure if you wanted to sprinkle all over your plate.

Okay, he admitted. So he'd always known he and Gail weren't destined to be a "forever" kind of couple—Tim had never felt "forever" about anyone. But still...

Dumped.

By a woman who had put "ha-ha" into her letter twice. He didn't care for the hollow feeling in the pit of his stomach—not in the least.

"How do you like that?" he muttered. Then said, "Damn," as hurt and anger rose to fill the hollow place. How could she? How dared she? He'd busted butt to get here, had left the Bay Area radio station he managed and the juicy scandal about the city council, just because Gail had asked him to.

And what had he wound up with? A roomful of people who couldn't find a date. Singles Anonymous. The Lonely Hearts Club.

What he ought to do was march right into that room and replace Gail in five seconds. She would be sorry she took off like that.

Expelling a deep breath, he felt his mouth curve up in a self-mocking grin. Come off it, Pelham, he said to himself. You're sounding pretty childish right about now. It was the hurt talking, of course. Hell, after the shock receded, he had a feeling he wouldn't even be that eager to replace Gail. He needed some time alone, for a change. Time without a woman.

Alone.

That hollow feeling in his gut came back. No, he didn't really want to be alone. Not tonight, anyway. He could stop in for a couple of quick ones at Sully's, talk about the upcoming 'Niners game with some of the regulars. Guys, most of them; very few women went there. Just guys sounded great right about now. Then he would—

"Mr. Pelham? We're about to start."

Startled, Tim glanced at the registration lady—Liz, her name tag said—and offered a rueful smile. "Sorry. I was woolgathering."

Liz pursed her lips, reminding Tim of his sixth-grade teacher, the one who let him know nothing he did got past her. "It's getting late. If you're going in, please do so now. The instructor is about to enter the room."

He eyed the orange booklet in his hand and chuckled. "Oh, yeah. The dating class. Um, I don't think I—''

Something at the edge of his vision grabbed his attention before he finished his sentence. He turned to see a woman walking slowly down the hallway toward him. Medium height. Carrot red hair. Nice face. Severe gray suit. Great legs.

And a walk that would stop traffic on the autobahn.

A slight sway, kind of a mesmerizing, full-hipped, rolling motion. Sensual as all get-out, but not on purpose or forced, he would bet on it. A naturally, unconsciously sexy female. He felt himself stand a little taller; if he'd been wearing a tie, he would have straightened it.

The woman paused at a bulletin board and made a couple of adjustments to some sagging notices. As she did so, something tugged at his memory. Hold it a minute, Tim thought. There was something familiar about her, but he couldn't place it. Did he know her?

"Excuse me," he said to Liz. "Who is that walking down the hall?"

With a beaming smile of pride, she replied, "That's your instructor for this evening, Sarah Dann. We're so lucky to have her. She owns the school, and she doesn't usually teach, but she's filling in tonight. Now, Mr. Pelham, are you staying? If not, we'll be happy to refund your money or apply it to another class. Ms. Dann's policy is that you don't have to pay if you're not satisfied."

She reached for his booklet, but Tim wasn't ready to let it go. Sarah Dann began walking again, with more determination in her stride. When she arrived at the door, she glanced at him briefly—through him, he thought—and smiled impersonally. A smattering of freckles, he noted, on the bridge of a small wide nose. Full lips, gray green eyes, a slight frown between the brows. Troubled about something, he thought, and trying not to show it.

And most definitely known to him. From somewhere.

Tim watched her sashay through the doorway. The back was as good as the front, the rolling hips just wide enough to miss being fashionable, but who cared about fashion anyway? Sarah Dann, Liz had said. Sarah…

At the moment of recall, he froze, then whistled softly. His memory might be fuzzy on some of the details, but oh, yeah, he knew her. Their single previous encounter had left a strong impression.

Sarah. She'd changed. A lot. But then, it had been a while, hadn't it? They'd both changed.

Well, well, he thought, strolling into the classroom, his mood suddenly altered for the better. The question of what to do with the rest of the evening had just been decided— he would attend an adult-education class on dating, of course. He had nothing better to do. And he was as free as the proverbial bird, thank you very much. Thanks to Gail and her motorcycle adventure.

In fact, Gail who?

As she crossed the threshold, Sarah continued the silent pep talk she'd been giving herself for the past few hours, cautioning herself to guard against moving her lips as she did. Lately, she'd been talking to herself—and answering back—which was not a sign of inner serenity, for sure. She figured as long as she didn't do it in public, she was still this side of the funny farm.

She could do this, she assured herself. She could teach this class. Rah. Rah. She *would* do this, and she would do it well. After all, she was a professional. She plastered a self-confident expression on her face, even as a small inner voice whispered that it would be nice to be somewhere else. Anywhere else.

The nervous chatter of her students filled the room. "I'm never letting Teddy fix me up again. I don't know if it's because he's gay or what, but he keeps saying *he* would go out with him."

"She was the daughter of a friend of my Aunt Frieda's from Poughkeepsie. This chick keeps quoting *The Nation* to me and I'm a *People* kind of guy."

"Is there a neon sign on my head that says Nerds and Weirdos Welcome?"

War stories, Sarah thought. Tales from the singles scene. She had a few of her own. She straightened her papers on the lectern, then glanced at her watch. This needn't be that big a deal. Relax and get on with it, she told herself for maybe the hundredth time. After all, she'd created Dating For Destiny five years before, and it had been a winner from the beginning—one that had contributed to the success of Keep On Learning.

But she no longer taught it. In fact, she'd planned never to have to teach it again. Unfortunately, earlier that day, the regular instructor had wrapped her car around a lamppost while swerving to avoid a cat. The cat was just dandy, but the instructor was in a cast, removed from civilized society for at least two months.

Ah, well, as her mother used to say, time to grin and bear it. After absentmindedly smoothing several strands of hair back into her French twist, Sarah felt them escape to freedom immediately. It was hopeless; her hair was a mess, as was her life. However, it was time to get this show on the road. Raging insecurity or not, downtime in her life or not, she was committed to getting through the next three hours and giving the students their money's worth. And, Sarah thought, resolutely straightening her shoulders and hoping the movement didn't make her blouse gap in the middle of her chest, their money's worth they would get.

"Hi, everyone," she said brightly, letting her glance take in the entire room. There were over forty people; a mixed group—all ages, all degrees of attractiveness. "You'll find notebooks and pens in front of you, and if you haven't put on your name tag, please do so now."

"Do we have to?" one woman whined. "I hate those things."

"No, you don't have to do a thing. But if you really came here to learn how to meet someone, lesson number one is that we have to be able to bend a bit to get what we want. If we're prickly or private or shy, we'll have to work just a little harder, make some adjustments, allow people in. And name tags are a good start."

"Do I have to put it on my sweater?"

"Put it on your forehead, if you want," Sarah said with a grin. "It'll be a great conversation opener. 'Excuse me, is that a name tag on your head or are you a prototype for a new species?'"

The members of the class chuckled appreciatively, and Sarah felt that thick core of inner tension begin to melt. She would be okay. All she had to remember was to crack some jokes, listen, and follow the course outline. She'd written it herself, hadn't she? She knew it worked.

Easing herself away from the safety of the lectern, she leaned a hip against the edge of the adjacent desk. "First off, let me tell you this. Following all the steps I've outlined will not guarantee that you'll find the love of your life, but it will increase the field of choices several times over. What happens is that you deal in volume. Specifically, *quality* volume.

"That special someone does not come riding up on a horse at sunset, does not spring from the pages of a magazine and sweep us up in his or her arms."

"He doesn't?" a girl called out, and there were more chuckles.

Sarah smiled. "Sorry. It's up to us to make it happen. There are places to go, things to do, classes to take and situations to find yourself in so that you meet lots of appropriate, available people, and one of those may very well be the one you've been dreaming about. If it sounds like hard work, it is."

When a couple of people groaned, Sarah said, "But worth it, trust me. When women go shopping for a dress, we usually go to several stores and try on many different styles before we find the right one. It might take a while, but when we do, well, look out." Grinning, she raised her hands in a "Ta-da!" gesture. "We're gorgeous, right?

"However, if we never go to the store in the first place, we never get the dress, never look the way we want to. So it is with relationships and love."

Several of her students nodded, a few looked uncomfortable, others just plain unhappy. Par for the course. Sarah's gaze again swept the room, stopping briefly at a man sitting way in the back, passed on, then jerked back to him again.

He'd been at the door earlier. Did she know him? She didn't think so, but why did he seem so familiar? He was in his late thirties, she estimated, with longish sandy brown hair, sprinkled lightly with silver. His face was nice, Sarah thought, with sleepy, sexy eyes that had lots of smile lines radiating outward. There was a faint five o'clock shadow over a firm chin and jawline—just enough to make him rugged looking. He wore a navy blue crew-neck sweater over a white shirt; his body was broad, but athletic rather than fat.

She couldn't shake her first impression that she knew him. But it was her second impression that bothered her—she found him extremely attractive, with his comfortable, understated masculinity that managed to draw the eye like a magnet. He was the kind of man you hoped to sit next to at a boring dinner party or bump into in the grocery line. A blind date from the gods. This one certainly should have no trouble meeting anyone.

She fiddled with the middle button on her blouse while she considered her third impression, which was surprise—at herself. No man had drawn her attention for a long while, and she was not thrilled by this reaction.

Turning her gaze away from the stranger she concentrated her attention on the others. Begone, man person, she ordered silently. No sir, no way, never again. End of discussion.

"Now," Sarah continued aloud, focusing her mind where it belonged, "let's check out my little course-outline booklet here, item by item. I hope you find it fun, and feel free to shout out questions as they come up. By the way, my name is Sarah and I'm not wearing a name tag because I hate them." She grinned again. "One of the perks of being the teacher."

Slouching in his chair at the rear of the room, Tim nodded and gave Sarah's lecturing technique his silent stamp of approval. She was good—positive and honest and human at the same time. Amazing. She'd been so different before. Night-and-day different. Withdrawn and tentative. Back then, had he even seen that sunny smile? He tried to remember.

He knew he was staring blatantly at her, but he couldn't seem to exercise his usual subtlety. A crucial button on her pale lace blouse kept threatening to dissociate itself from the buttonhole and he found that downright fascinating. She probably thought the austere cut of the suit jacket hid her assets, but what it did instead—for him, anyway—was to make her more tantalizing.

He wanted her, he realized with a start; really wanted her.

Being physically attracted to a woman wasn't unusual, but this was more of an instantaneous turn-on; a real kick in the pants, so to speak. The strength of his reaction took him aback. After all, he was no longer a kid with raging hormones, but that was how he felt.

Hold it, he cautioned himself. This could be a rebound reaction to Gail's little stunt; the chest-beating male of the species asserting his power after having it threatened.

But it sure didn't feel that way. It felt more like...old business, somehow.

Unfinished old business.

*Powerful* unfinished old business.

The next step was obvious—he would make sure he connected with Sarah this evening. He hoped she would respond the way he wanted her to. He knew he was acceptable looking and an okay guy. Maybe a little too dedicated to his job and football. But he did all right with the ladies.

In fact, there was a joke around the station—one that always caused him a twinge of embarrassment—that Tim had invented some kind of animal-scent after-shave that sent subliminal messages to all the available, premenopausal, heterosexual women within the radius of a block, so they ran over each other to get to him.

It was an exaggeration, of course; a major exaggeration. But still, the truth was he liked women and they liked him. He had rarely been without one in his life.

"How many of you are willing to make romance a priority?" Sarah asked.

The question brought Tim's musings to a halt. Priority? "How many of you," she continued, "are willing to, say, for four weeks, make finding someone special the most important thing in your life?''

A few tentative hands went up; the others looked around in discomfort.

''All right, how many would make a diet guaranteed to drop twenty pounds a priority for four weeks?'' There were some chuckles, more raised hands. ''How about taking a course having to do with your career that would guarantee a promotion and more money and more satisfaction, and all it would require is four weeks out of your life?''

More hands, laughter. ''So, tell me, why won't we make finding love a priority? Any suggestions?''

''Well,'' said a young woman in the row in front of Tim, ''it's kind of, you know, embarrassing.''

''Yeah,'' a man piped up. ''It's like having to admit, here I am on a search—like, you shouldn't have to do that, it should just happen.''

''People will think there's something wrong with you if you have to work that hard to find someone,'' said another. ''That you're needy.''

Sarah smiled her understanding. ''I used to feel the same, and let me assure you there's nothing wrong with anyone. We live in different times. Courting rituals have changed, we're having to invent new ones. Where did you used to meet people? In school. At work. Family friends. Parties, casual encounters, blind dates. But if you're no longer in school, if you work for a small business or for yourself, if your family is scattered all over the place and your friends don't throw parties, what's left is casual encounters, and I don't mean the bar scene.''

Someone groaned and Sarah nodded. ''Right, that's okay for some people, but mostly you don't wind up with a long-term romance when you meet in a bar. And nowadays, you might wind up with a lot of things you don't want.

''Okay, then, there's the video store, the market, the post

office. Bookstores. But who are these people we meet casually? What do we know about them?"

She was really good, Tim thought once again. A natural speaker. One who made you use your gray matter.

Just how much priority would he give to romance? He'd never considered it before. His usual pattern was to be, as the saying went, "serially monogamous"—one woman at a time, no cheating. Laughs and lots of rumpled sheets, nothing too serious. Had he, somewhere in the back of his mind, thought about finding something deeper? Maybe a wife? Doing the whole kids-and-sheepdog routine?

His childhood spent as a motherless army brat hadn't exactly provided a shining example, but he'd seen it work a couple of times. Had he ever dreamed of it, or wished for it? In all honesty? Maybe. Once in a while.

But had it ever been a priority? Nope.

"Okay." Sarah pushed herself away from the desk and walked back and forth in front of it. "Now comes the fun part. Please open your blank pads and make three columns. At the top of the first, write 'Must Have.' The second is 'Will Settle.' And the third is 'Deal Breakers.'

"The first list, obviously, is those qualities you require in a mate. You absolutely would not even look twice unless he or she had them—that may be religious affiliation, money, height for some people, sense of humor. One woman I know was adamant that she would never date anyone whose name didn't begin with a *J*." She raised an eyebrow suggestively. "Something to do with a witch and a Ouija board, I believe she said."

After a couple of chuckles from the class, she went on. "The next, 'Will Settle,' is fairly obvious. You'd rather he or she had this quality—blond hair, golf nut, movie buff, night owl or early riser, that kind of thing—but if not, you're not going to lose too much sleep over it.

"And the last, 'Deal Breakers,' is also, I think, fairly

obvious. If you cannot tolerate lactovegetarians or men with black nose hair or born-again nudists or even people who sing off-key, that goes on the list. Everybody got it?''

She looked around the room, but it seemed to Tim that she avoided settling her gaze on him. ''Take the next five minutes,'' Sarah instructed, ''and fill up those columns.''

''Five minutes?'' a man asked. ''I'll need five years.''

When Sarah joined in the general laughter that greeted his remark, Tim sat up straight in his chair.

That laugh.

A deep, rich sound that gave new meaning to the word *lusty*—one that brought the memory into sharper focus. Much sharper. Yes. It came back to him now in its entirety.

Fourteen...no, fifteen years ago. Another school, another classroom. The skinny, terrified girl with wild red hair; the one who had turned him on, then turned him down.

The one that got away.

2

While in his senior year in high school, Tim had lost his dad to a heart attack. The old man hadn't been much of a father, but he'd been the only family Tim had known. After graduation, feeling lost and directionless, he'd signed up for the navy. He took to it right away, to the regimentation of training and the freedom from restraint during liberty. When his shipmates had awarded him the nickname of "The Ploughman," he'd been pleased. At eighteen, he'd considered himself something of a stud and proud of it.

Four years later, when he decided to quit the navy and go back to school, he was older and no longer cared for the nickname. He enrolled in San Francisco State University on the GI Bill. At twenty-two and still a little on the cocky side, Tim had long hair and a beard, and dreams of being an actor. That had been fifteen years ago.

The day he'd met Sarah had been his first time attending the drama department's Scene Study class. The two of them were paired to read and rehearse a scene from Tennessee Williams's play, *Cat on a Hot Tin Roof*—the one between Brick and Maggie in their bedroom. Maggie was supposed to be dressed in a sexy slip and not much else, and at that point in the play, was all fired up and restless with unfulfilled sexual longing.

Tim took one look at the partner he'd been assigned—at her pale young face, her high-necked blouse, modest skirt and loafers, her lack of anything even remotely suggesting a burning, sensual inner life—and had serious doubts about the casting.

In truth, he found the girl singularly *un*-sexy. Her hands shook with nerves, and her body was thin and bony—not in the least curvaceous. Large, frightened eyes refused to meet his as they were introduced. How in hell was he expected to play off her as though she were the very Goddess of Temptation herself? he wondered, not real happy with the assignment.

They read through the scene once, and his unhappiness grew. He knew he had a lot to learn about acting, but this girl was as wooden as a bench. Then they stood, started blocking and working on it, and in those next couple of hours, a miracle happened. Somehow, the girl was transformed.

Her gray green eyes were no longer terrified, but seemed o have changed into something more, well, catlike. Her nhibitions lessened, then she lost them altogether, as she slowly evolved into the sensual, earthy woman that was Maggie. If her body remained tense, it was now with longing, not fear. She circled him as he stood, transfixed; she slunk, she prowled, she nearly purred.

Even though she was totally covered by her clothing, Tim had no trouble picturing her in a revealing white slip, imagining the points of her breasts jutting against the silk fabric, a pink flush of awareness all over her neck.

His character, Brick, was supposed to be unaffected by Maggie's allure, but Tim had a difficult time pretending disinterest. As the rehearsal time lengthened, and they made more and more eye contact, there rose between them a heightened responsiveness, a growing heat. For him, it was foreplay unlike any he'd ever experienced. By the time the two hours were over, his loins were hard and throbbing with wanting her, and the sailor-tight fit of his jeans wasn't making it any easier.

Afterward, without speaking, they picked up their books and walked out of the classroom together, their arms just brushing against each other's. He adjusted the straps of his backpack while she held her large satchel clutched tightly to her chest, as though needing a shield. The blush on her cheeks was either a matching turned-on reaction or embarrassment at feeling it, but, Tim decided, there was no doubt that what was uppermost in her mind was the same as what was in his. No doubt at all.

They made their way down the hallway in taut silence, the heat still hovering about them like steam from a shower, until Tim couldn't bear it anymore. Taking her by the shoulders, he turned her to face him.

"How about we go back to my place and finish this up?" he asked softly.

"Finish it up?" she echoed, as though she had no idea what he was talking about.

"What we started back there, during the rehearsal. This…thing between us."

Her eyes widened; she looked like the proverbial doe caught in the glare of headlights. Her nostrils flared slightly, but she bit her bottom lip and was silent. Maggie was gone now. The student was back.

He let go of her shoulders. He'd been too straightforward, Tim realized, gazing at her full, almost-pouty mouth that he hadn't noticed until they'd begun to rehearse. He wanted her—wanted her bad—but this one needed gentleness, loosening up. Forcing his body into a more relaxed stance, he leaned back against the wall and gazed down at her rosy face.

Offering a small, quasi-apologetic smile, he asked, "Or am I being too blunt? Would you prefer I said something along the lines of 'Why don't we get to know each other better?' A lot better,'' he added, capturing her green-eyed gaze.

"Oh." Her full lips formed a circle. Other students hurried by, but Tim kept focused on her. Again worrying the edge of her lower lip with her teeth, she said, "Sorry. I can't."

"Got a hot date?" he teased.

Without answering, she looked down at her feet.

"Hey," he said quietly. He lifted her chin with his index finger and made her meet his eyes. "Hey," he said again, "I didn't imagine what went on in there, did I?"

A moment passed, then she expelled a breath. "No, you didn't imagine it."

Score one for her for admitting it, he thought, letting his hand drop to his side. A lot of women would have pulled the coy "Whatever do you mean?" response.

Maybe she needed to be courted, slowly and methodically. Maybe, for her, sex was less like a terrific, feel-good itch that required immediate scratching, and more of an *emotional* thing. Men and women were different, he'd found out, most especially in the area of physical love.

"Busy tomorrow night?" Tim asked. "Or Sunday? We could go to a movie, or have dinner, if you don't mind spaghetti and cheap wine. I'm talking *real* cheap. Like in Thunderbird, only not as good."

She laughed then. It was the damnedest sound—low and throaty and raspy, like a woman luxuriating in bed with her lover. The sound took him by surprise. It absolutely did not go with this girl.

He felt his jeans getting uncomfortable again.

"God, you have a great laugh," he said.

"No, don't." She shook her head. "You really mustn't do this. All this—" She made a gesture with one hand that meant she didn't have the words.

But he knew; he was pushing again. He wished his body would stop pushing him. "Getting to you, am I? Good."

"No. Stop." She put her hand over his mouth as though to shut him up. Without thinking, he parted his lips and bit down gently on her fingers. Then he sucked on the tips, rolling his tongue back and forth over the soft pads. She drew in a surprised breath but made no move to remove her hand from his mouth, only watched in fascination as he used his lips and tongue and teeth on her skin.

She tasted sweet and delicate, and he sucked even harder. He heard her breathing quickening in concert with his. Then, all at once, her eyes widened as though realization had hit, and she snatched her hand away. Wiping her fingers on her skirt, she took off down the hallway.

He hurried after her, unable to keep from smiling. "Okay, I stopped."

She kept right on walking, her face straight ahead, so he said, "Well? Is it a date?"

"No." She shook her head.

"Tell me why."

"I can't."

He frowned. It wasn't that she was playing hard to get— no, there was something more. But he could see that he was making her uncomfortable. Was it worth it? Did he really want to work this hard? He should probably drop the whole thing.

For some reason, he didn't seem able to do that.

He compromised. "Well, all right then. I can be patient—" he grinned "—if it's not too long. I'll ask again. Soon."

She said nothing, so they continued along the busy, loud corridor toward the sunlight. He glanced at her briefly. "I guess I'll be seeing you on Monday, anyway, when we work on the scene again."

Again, she didn't respond, and he wondered what she

was chewing over in her head. Then, as though arriving at a decision, she stopped and faced him. "I don't think so. I won't be back. To the Scene Study class, I mean."

They were in the doorway to the open quad. Other students made their way around the two of them, but he didn't pay them any mind. Grabbing her upper arms, Tim said, "Hold it just a minute. You're not coming back? But we just spent two hours rehearsing."

"I know. I'm sorry. But you'll be able to replace me immediately, on Monday. I really am sorry. I'm not usually irresponsible, or flaky...."

She let the sentence trail off and looked away, toward a far-off building.

Her announcement had not only surprised him, but had hit his gut like a well-aimed punch. Realizing he was holding her too tightly, he let go of her arms and asked with strained lightness, "Hey, was it something I said? Do I have garlic breath?"

"Oh, no!" she said immediately, facing him again. "No. It's nothing to do with you. You're a very... Well, I think you know you're..." Again, she left her sentence unfinished; again, the flush rose on her cheeks.

Oh, yeah, he thought, his brief spurt of insecurity gone in an instant. She wanted him.

Was she a virgin? Was that the problem? Since high school, he hadn't had a lot of experience with virgins. Needless to say, she wouldn't be too thrilled if he asked her—not right here. "You can trust me," he said, meaning it. "I won't push you to, you know, do anything you don't want to do, if that's what this is about."

A wistful expression in her eyes pleaded for his understanding. "It's just that—" she swallowed again "—I'll be on my honeymoon next week. I'm getting married. This weekend. Tomorrow, as a matter of fact. Goodbye."

Then she'd run off, just like that, before he'd even gotten

a chance to say something clever like, "Getting married? Is that all?" Or, "Really? Then you deserve one last fling at freedom." He'd said nothing to her retreating back; only stared after her, his body still hard with longing and a curious twist of regret—pain?—in the area of his heart.

He tried to remember her name—hadn't paid attention when she'd introduced herself, and she'd never said it later. Something with an *S*. Susan? Sally? No. Sarah. Yeah, Sarah.

It didn't matter, though. To him, she was Maggie the Cat, and always would be.

He hadn't seen her again, but had thought of her once in a while over the years and had never understood why she still haunted him. Maggie the Cat. The one who had said no.

Tim gazed at the woman who had been that girl, this Sarah Dann, standing before him now. Her hair was not quite as vividly red as it had been then, but her mouth was still as luscious. She was more confident, of course. Funny, too. She'd revealed not a hint of a sense of humor back then, but he liked that she had one now. He liked especially the way her frame had filled out, even though the subtle way she kept adjusting her blouse over that iffy breast button let him know she might not be as pleased.

He checked her hands—no rings—then smiled to himself. Yes, sir, the evening was looking up. He wasn't even that bothered over Gail's rejection. Sure, no one liked being dumped, but, well, bless Gail for leaving. They'd been headed in that direction anyway. "When one door closes, another one opens," she used to say to him, parroting one of her "search for meaning" gurus.

In this case, he thought, Gail was right. As of tonight, Tim was unattached. The door was wide-open, waiting for him to invite Sarah in. Remembering the turned-on, yet regretful expression on her young face all those years ago, Tim thought there was a pretty fair chance she would step inside.

Sarah was on a roll. Heck, she was actually enjoying teaching again. Part of it was just being in the company of other human beings. She hadn't been very social lately. Instead, she'd become all too familiar with her television set and had seen every syndicated episode of "Law and Order" twice. It was a nice change, being among the living. She needed to do more of this. Besides, as cynical as she might be feeling about romance itself, the suggestions she made really worked. She knew that from personal experience.

She guided the class through the effectiveness of smiling, affirmations of their own worth, how to flirt without seeming desperate, and the importance of really listening to the other person instead of planning one's own next sentence. The members of her class were a bunch of lively people, and their reaction was gratifying.

Except for the man in the back; he didn't take part at all. He never took his eyes off her—which was unnerving, to say the least—and she couldn't shake the growing feeling that she knew him from somewhere; and that the memory was not a comfortable one.

Pushing these reflections away, Sarah perched on the edge of her desk and tugged at her blouse. "Okay, everyone, now we're going to practice a little."

Some groans were heard.

"Hey, come on. You proved you have courage by showing up tonight, so let's keep up the good work. You will get results, I promise.

"Now, please turn to the person next to you, if they're of the opposite sex. If not, find the closest person of the opposite sex and pair up. You have ten minutes. Stand up, sit down, take a walk, socialize. Introduce yourselves, find out about each other, interests, occupations. Flirt a little, smile, listen. Exchange cards if you have them or if you want to. Remember, this is just practice. There's nothing at stake.''

As her students found their partners, Sarah returned to the lectern and sorted through her notes, her mood totally altered from when she'd first entered the classroom. The hubbub of many conversations filled the room, and she felt good.

A tap on her shoulder made her look around. It was him, the one in the back.

"It seems we're one female short,'' he said. "What shall I do, teacher?''

His smile was a little lopsided and utterly charming, his eyes an incredibly clear, light blue. The sense of recognition was much stronger now; on the tip of her brain, like a familiar forgotten word that is just out of reach. There was something about his attitude, that seemingly calm self-confidence. But he was not a relaxed man; not through and through, not really. This close to him, she was able to pick up on the intensity just beneath the laid-back surface. The combination was lethal.

Where had she come into contact with this man before?

"I'm sorry,'' she said. "We try to make it even.''

He shrugged. "Can't count on everyone showing up, I guess. And I really do need to practice.''

Sure he did, she thought. Like the Pope needed to practice being Catholic. "Oh, well, then, I guess you'll have to make do with me.''

"I'll suffer through it if you will.'' His grin grew broader and she found herself returning it. He was irresistible.

She hated irresistible men. Sometimes, fate had a downright distorted sense of humor.

Offering his hand, he said, "I'm Tim Pelham.''

"Sarah Dann," she said, automatically returning the handshake. It was firm, his skin dry and warm. Then his name registered. "Tim? Tim Pelham, you said?"

With a little twist of a smile, he replied, "You remember, then. Maggie the Cat."

Anything resembling concentration flew out the window. She felt light-headed, panicked; her traitorous redhead's pale complexion heated up as though someone had turned on a furnace.

"I had no salt-and-pepper in my hair then," he continued, still holding her hand, "and a major beard. I was a lot skinnier, too. Shaggier. And pretty full of myself, as only the young can be. Remember?"

Did she remember? Oh, God. The student—years older than the rest of the freshman class, more worldly—who'd turned her entire life around. Did she remember? Had she ever forgotten?

Sarah found herself speechless, managing only to stare at him while her heart thumped rapidly. He was the one who finally let go of her hand. He leaned against the blackboard so that to face him, she had to turn her back to the rest of the room. Then he folded his arms across his chest and offered another lopsided grin. "Amazing, the twists and turns of life, huh?"

"Amazing, yes."

As though he sensed her discomfort, he graciously changed the subject. "I hear this is your school. You own it?"

"Yes."

"Congratulations. I'm impressed."

School. Career. And-what-do-you-do? type conversation. All right, Sarah thought. She could manage that. "Thank you," she said. "And you—are you still acting?"

He shook his head. "Naw. Never got very far. Not enough fire in the belly, I guess. I went into broadcasting.

Disc jockey, reporter, news director. I'm at KCAW Radio now—All News and Lots of Talk, Talk, Talk is our motto.''

"Yes, I'm familiar with it. What do you do there?"

He offered another easy shrug. "I'm the manager. Are you one of our listeners?"

"No. News depresses me. I prefer to listen to music in my car."

"Our sister station, KRNR, plays oldies rock."

"I like classical."

"Ah."

The conversation ran out of steam at that point. Wildly searching her blank mind for another topic, Sarah opened her mouth to say, "Well—"

But Tim beat her to it. "So, what do you think? Us being such old friends and all, want to have a cup of coffee after the class?"

*Uh-oh.* Her back stiffened automatically and large warning bells ding-donged in her head. She took a moment to compose herself, then said, "Good. That's the right idea." Continuing to hide behind her teacher persona, she continued, "You should have no problem initiating conversations with women, Mr. Pelham. Women other than me, of course."

He studied her for the flicker of a moment. "Tim," he corrected. "And why 'of course'?"

"Because I'm the teacher tonight," she said crisply. "This is practice, not reality. But you're a natural. I'll bet you already know a lot more than I could even begin to teach."

*Uh-oh,* again. She'd let a tiny edge of sarcasm creep into that last sentence, but it had just slipped out. And it was too late to take it back now.

Turning around to face the classroom again, Sarah clapped her hands to be heard above the din. "Hello?" she called out. "The ten minutes are up. How'd it go?"

The reactions varied from enthusiastic to grumbling, with details. Instead of returning to his seat in the back, Tim slid into one in the front row, making him impossible to ignore. She was aware of him the way you always knew when someone was about to snap your picture. You might try to act naturally, but there was no way you could.

"How about some more?" she asked with desperate cheer. "It's time to switch partners. Grab another man or woman, whoever's closest. Remember, this is only practice—you don't have to get all worried about how you're going over, or if you're saying the wrong thing. That's what practicing is for, to make mistakes and learn from them."

The chaos began again as people paired off. A man lumbered up to Sarah. He was quite tall, with a large belly, and she had a quick mental image of being crushed beneath him. Out of the corner of her eye, she observed a woman with very short black hair and a body from a workout-machine catalog grabbing Tim and saying, "Zap, you're mine!"

Grinning mock helplessness at Sarah, he allowed himself to be led off to a corner, to "practice" some more.

Sarah's new partner wasted no time telling her all about his successful recruiting business and the new office he was opening up and the brand-new BMW—a convertible, chuckle chuckle—he'd just leased because leasing was such sound business practice...blah-blah-blah.

Sarah nodded, listening with one ear to this pompous, self-absorbed giant, who was probably a marshmallow inside but you would need the patience of a saint to find it. She had no trouble understanding why he was here tonight; his people skills needed a major overhaul.

What she did have trouble understanding was why she'd felt that spurt of red-hot jealousy when Tim was claimed by the black-haired *bitch* with the body beautiful.

Dear God, Sarah thought, nodding again at the new Bimmer owner. Bitch? Where in the world had that come from? Even though her nature was a fairly volatile one, she'd been emotionally shut down for a while, and the strength of this reaction, the venom directed at the other woman, the downright *possessiveness* she'd felt about Tim, was dismaying.

What was she doing? She'd sworn off jealousy, she'd sworn off dating, she'd sworn off the male half of the human race. This was an aberration, and a far-from-welcome one.

During the coffee break, Sarah retreated to the safety of her office where she shuffled some papers, then spent more time than necessary in the ladies' room. By the time the second half of the class resumed, she was cool and collected again, her messy emotions tamped down by resolve.

She noted that Tim had returned to his original seat at the back of the classroom, but the formerly isolated row was now occupied by a string of women in chairs on either side of him. How cute. His own little harem. Why was she not surprised?

To his credit, he didn't give Sarah one of those "See what you're missing?" looks, the way a lot of men might; instead, he smiled charmingly at the members of his new "henhouse," then turned his complete attention back to Sarah and her every word.

Oh, boy, was he good. A master. She swatted him out of her mind like a pesky fly and put all her concentration on the next part of the class. The Action Plan. She went through the four-week daily diary, including morning and evening affirmations, going on practice dates with platonic friends, trying out new places, eventually risking and accepting rejection.

Her class handout included all kinds of helpful information on writing personal ads, navigating computer bulletin boards, matchmaking services, singles clubs formed around specific interests. She fielded questions from her students with good humor, observing with satisfaction that the tense and anxious—and lonely—individuals who had entered the room three hours ago had gradually formed into a cohesive group of people on a mission. She had done her job.

"If anyone's interested," she said in conclusion, "there is a Dating For Destiny Follow-Up Plan. It's a data base of all former students, and if you'd like to be included, we do a little matchmaking—for a small fee, of course. There are forms to fill out on the registration table, or you can call the school tomorrow." This service had proved to be an unexpected financial success; Sarah employed a full-time person whose only job was to co-ordinate the data base and make phone calls.

"So, that's all I have to say. It's been delightful meeting all of you this evening. Thank you."

"Sarah?" One of the students—a young man who had Computer Technician written all over him, from his stringy hair to the plaid short-sleeved shirt to the five ballpoint pens in his pocket—had his hand raised in the air. "The truth now. Does this actually work?"

Sarah leaned back against the desk, propped her fists on her hips and said, "You'd better believe it works. It's how I met my fiancé."

# 3

**S**arah's announcement was greeted with raucous, good-natured appreciation from all—except Tim. What? he asked silently. Fiancé? No. Not fair. He and Sarah had met twice, and both times she was on her way to tying herself to someone else. No wonder she'd given him the brush-off tonight. She wasn't available. Again.

Not that she was married yet. Engaged was pretty close, though. And he had a hands-off policy as far as other men's women were concerned.

But if she was engaged, why didn't she wear a ring, like everyone else did?

The general buzz of excitement in the room interrupted his train of thought. People were packing up to leave. The class was over. A couple of women nearby smiled at him, one nervously and one confidently, and with breathless little laughs, offered their cards to him. He thanked them both, apologized for not having his business cards with him, and said something vague about calling. Which he would not. Hell, he hadn't wanted to be here in the first place. He felt really let down, out of sorts, not a happy camper.

He caught himself before he began to snarl out loud. Come off it, Pelham, he told himself. He was being a grouch. You win some, you lose some. Sure, it hadn't been a great night. Between Gail and Sarah, he'd been rejected twice. But he was a pretty decent rebounder. What he would do was rush right on back to the station and cheer-lead his reporters on the city hall scandal. The evening's disappointments would be forgotten in no time.

To work, pronto, he told himself as he hopped up from his seat, brushed past the others and headed out the door. Work. Always the best cure for whatever ailed you. Then home to bed.

Alone.

Yes. Best thing all around.


When the last of the students had said their goodbyes, Sarah slumped against the edge of the desk and, for the first time in three hours, allowed herself to let down. She kicked off her heels and unzipped the top of her skirt just a little where it pinched.

She felt out of sorts. She was fifteen pounds overweight, thanks to the recent disintegration of her love life and the attendant nibbling that went with it. Several strands of her hair were caught in her eyelashes and she tried to smooth them back into her collapsing French twist.

How had she had the audacity to counsel other people on affairs of the heart? What did she know, except how to choose Mr. Wrong?

Thanks to the success of tonight's class, at least the rat-tat-tat of self-disapproval she'd been experiencing lately was no longer pounding in her head; no, it had transferred to the back of her neck, thank you very much. Sarah rubbed at the tight muscles with her fingers, ruefully congratulating herself on the acting job she'd just done. Her students had gotten their money's worth, that was for sure, even if she had used up her entire yearly allotment of cheer.

Closing her eyes, she let out a huge sigh. What a fraud she was. What a total, complete, hypocritical—

"I see it hits your neck, too."

Her eyes flew open and she angled her body toward the

doorway. She hadn't heard anyone approaching, but Tim Pelham stood there, leaning against the doorjamb, his hands in his pockets, a cool, impersonal look in his eyes.

"Excuse me?" she said, surreptitiously yanking up her skirt zipper and feeling around the floor for her heels.

"Tension. It usually goes to the neck or the lower back. You and I both got the neck, lucky us. Leave your shoes where they are. Here."

The next thing she knew, he had perched a hip next to hers on the desktop, taken her by the shoulders, and turned her so her back was to him. Gently, he eased her head down till her chin was resting on her chest, then with both hands began to massage the tightness from her neck and shoulders.

"I... Uh..." she managed, thinking she ought to protest somehow. But the man had incredibly strong fingers. And the thumbs—God, the thumbs!

"Shh," Tim said. "Let me. I'm good at this."

He certainly was. The man with the magic hands. Sarah turned her mind off because she not only didn't have the strength to fight, she had no inclination to do so at the moment. She let herself luxuriate in the firm strokes he applied in exactly the right places, and felt the knots giving way under his insistent pressure.

She had no idea how long her impromptu massage lasted, because she no longer occupied her body. She was floating somewhere else—nearby, in a land of fantasy.

She heard someone in the room groan and realized it had come from her very own self, so she groaned again. "Oh, you don't know how good that feels."

"We aim to please."

Uh-huh. She'd already figured that out. Pleasure was Tim Pelham's middle name. Her mind drifted some more. She wouldn't put up much of a fuss if he and his hands wanted to do this often. All over, actually. You could tell a lot about a person by how they touched you, and Tim was downright gifted, tuned in to her, sensual, strong.

He would be an A Number One lover, she imagined, and a generous one. Not in a hurry. Slow hands, as the song went. Confident hands. Especially with those thumbs. Maybe if she couldn't have the hands, the thumbs would—

*Hold it,* came the warning voice. Wherever in the world was her imagination heading? Up the wrong pathway in the brain, for sure.

"Thanks," she said brightly as she straightened and jumped off the desk. Scooting her feet into her shoes, Sarah faced him. "All better now."

He seemed amused by her obvious falsehood, but shrugged as he said, "Not really, but...whatever."

Briskly gathering her papers into piles, she asked, "Did you forget something? Is that why you came back?"

He seemed to be studying her for a silent few moments, then folded his arms over his chest. One corner of his mouth quirked up. "Actually, I wanted to apologize for coming on a little strong, you know, earlier. It seemed like such a nice coincidence, seeing you again after all these years. And, well, I didn't know you were...taken. Like they say, déjà vu all over again. So, I came back to say I'm sorry."

"That's thoughtful of you, but there's nothing to apologize for."

He looked as though he wanted to say something else, but instead pushed himself off the desk. She watched as he ambled thoughtfully toward the door. Then he stopped abruptly and turned around.

"So, what do you think?" he asked. "How about, for old times' sake, you and I actually do go out for a cup of coffee?" His hands came up as though to ward off protests. "And I promise, no coming on. Just friends."

Oh, Lord, Sarah thought, her head back to its previously swirling, confused state as she stared at him. That crooked smile, the small squint lines at the corners of his killer-blue eyes, as though he spent his days sailing. Her glance took in that solid, compact body of his, the way his thigh muscles bulged in his jeans, the broadness of his hands. Not super tall—under six feet, probably—but one-hundred-percent man.

A basically nice man, Sarah added with the objective part of her mind that was still working. And completely aware of his effect on women. No doubt about it.

She had to be grateful he'd bought the fiancé line—and why shouldn't he? Sarah had been unengaged for six months now, but she had indeed met Charles in this class. He'd approached her, not unlike Tim, and asked her out, and she'd said yes. The rest, as the saying went, was history.

Past history. She might have found her fiancé this way, but she'd since lost him. Those who can, do. Those who can't, teach.

She voiced none of these thoughts, however. Some self-protective mechanism warned her not to inform Tim that she was no longer "taken." Even if fifteen years had passed since they'd first met, he still felt somehow dangerous to her.

Back then, that amazing attraction, to someone she barely knew, had turned her safe world upside down. It had made her run for her life, quit a class she'd been looking forward to, then drop out of college entirely; it had brought up all kinds of doubts about herself and her feelings toward the man she was to marry. Those doubts had been with her on her wedding day and had only grown stronger in the five years that followed.

She'd been so very young. It had been a mistake to marry, but she'd been a dutiful daughter, an only child and a "good" girl whose elderly parents had urged her to accept a proposal from a man ten years older. A "safe" man with a good job; a man, they assured her, she would grow to love. At eighteen, she'd not yet learned to make her own decisions. She'd not yet learned a lot of things.

Such as the way her body could go up in flames in the presence of a near stranger. Tim Pelham. From the moment they'd been introduced, she'd desired—no, *craved* him, all of him. After two hours in his presence, during which she'd discovered in herself a freedom and sensuality she hadn't known existed, the craving was even more intense. And more threatening.

So she'd made the snap decision not to return to the class. To never see Tim again, if she could help it. She'd run from the temptation he represented as though running for her very life. And, in fact, she had not set eyes on him again.

Until tonight.

She told herself sternly to keep Tim just where she'd kept him fifteen years ago—at arm's length. Not only was she still not fully recovered from Charles's betrayal, nor in the market for a new lover, but she knew—she just *knew*, in her gut—that this man understood all about lust and not a lot about love. Like Charles. He would let her down, the way Charles had; even break her heart. And she really didn't want to go through that again. Enough was enough.

So she didn't correct his impression of her marital status, instead casually replying to his invitation with, "Not tonight, thanks. It's been a long day and I need to get home."

"Another time?"

"I'm pretty busy."

Again he studied her without speaking. Then she saw him decide to back off and was grateful, because part of her was screaming at the other part to, for heaven's sake, have a cup of coffee with the man. What could it hurt?

"All right," he said easily. "I'll walk you to your car."

"I have to close up my office."

"Fine with me."

Why had he come back? Tim wondered as he accompanied Sarah down the hall. And why in hell was he still here? His behavior was totally out of character. He was never this aggressive when interested in a woman. His style was more laid-back, more about letting it happen without working too hard. And, in this instance, he so clearly was not wanted.

All he knew was that there was this strange, fierce pull toward Sarah Dann, this reluctance to let her out of his sight, even in the face of her pretty emphatic rebuff.

She filed some papers, turned out the lights and locked the door, then they went out the school's back entrance. The night was cool, the color of the autumn leaves barely discernible in the shadowy light of the parking lot.

"I love this time of year," Tim said, taking a deep breath, "especially up here in northern California."

"Yes, I do, too."

"Are you native?"

"One of the rare ones, yes. You?"

He chuckled. "Hardly. We lived in seventeen different states, but I'm told I was born in a base hospital in Honolulu. My dad was in the military."

"Is he still around?"

"No, he died a long time ago. Where's your car?"

"Way in the back by those cypresses."

As they strolled toward her car, he noticed that Sarah kept a careful distance between them, almost as though she'd wrapped herself in an invisible cocoon.

The school was situated at the edge of a medium-size mall, and the other stores were closed. The two of them were alone. The night was quiet, except for the clicking of her high heels and the distant roar of freeway traffic. Tim felt vaguely unsettled, ill at ease with the barrier Sarah had put up.

"That's quite a class you teach there," he said after a while.

"Thanks. I don't usually run it, not anymore. I was filling in tonight."

"Oh, yeah, that's right. Who came up with all that stuff?"

"I did, actually. I think it works pretty well. I'm pleased."

He heard the quiet pride in her voice and smiled. "You should be. It's well organized and interesting. Plus, you're a gifted teacher."

Wrinkling her nose, as though embarrassed by the compliment, she said, "It's the ham in me, I think. It doesn't get much chance to come out. Nowadays, running the school takes most of my time and teaching almost none."

"I've got a little of that ham in me, too. Not quite the lampshade-on-the-head-at-parties kind, but there have been times—" He left the sentence unfinished, chuckling instead. "I suppose that's why we both enrolled in the drama class. Did you want to be an actress?"

"No. I took it because I thought it would help me to be less...stiff in front of people. Less tongue-tied."

"Interesting. So here we are, the two of us, all these years later, both of us in management, not acting. Who'd have thought it? Did you marry that guy?"

She looked startled. "Excuse me?"

"You said you were getting married that weekend. You know, after we rehearsed, after you were Maggie the Cat."

"Oh. Yes, I did."

He debated a follow-up question, but decided to leave the ball in her court. Which she took up, offering, "We're divorced. It lasted five years."

"Any kids?"

"No."

"Me neither."

She glanced over at him. "Have you ever married?"

"Never."

She smiled. "That sounds kind of emphatic."

"Yeah. I guess so." He scratched his head. "I don't know, I don't seem to get involved with women I can picture waking up next to every morning for the rest of my life."

"What kind of women do you get involved with? If that's not too personal."

"No, it's okay." Tim took a moment to think about it. Mostly, they were models, actresses, divorcées with a lot of time on their hands and not enough to do. "Women who want to have too much fun to settle down, I guess."

"Are the two mutually exclusive?"

He grinned at her. "Beats me. Never tried it."

And never would, Sarah was sure. She congratulated herself as they walked along. She'd been right on the money. Tim was the perfect Peter Pan, at least where women were concerned. All play, no responsibility. Eternal youth. He was—what?—thirty-seven? Thirty-eight? And had never married. Never taken that kind of mature step.

She knew all about men with his stats. There was a hole somewhere in the middle of their souls. They ought to wear a sign saying, Warning: Approach with Caution. Or better yet, Do Not Approach at All.

"Well—" she fiddled in her purse for her keys "—here's my car."

He whistled in admiration at her low-slung Mazda Miata. "Hey, nice. I don't see you as the red-convertible type."

"Oh? What type am I?"

Narrowing his eyes, he studied her face. "Dark blue, or silver, small four-door, lots of trunk room, with great pickup. You like to burn rubber at intersections."

Sarah's mouth fell open in genuine surprise. "I can't believe this. That was the car I traded in for this one. That's amazing."

He offered up that crooked grin, that no-big-deal shrug again. "It's just something I do. I get these feelings about people sometimes. Like I know them—kind of a mind link."

"And you know me?"

"Well, I know you have a terrific sense of humor—"

"Thank you."

"And you tend to be impatient, mostly with yourself, I think. And you're shy inside, but you've managed to overcome it."

"I stuttered as a child."

"There. You see? And you work hard—probably way too hard—and don't let yourself play very often."

Sarah rested a hip against the driver's door and stared at him. "Didn't you say you managed a radio station? On the side, do you do crystal-ball readings? Or maybe you have your own show. You know, 'Dr. Pelham's Psychic Help Line.'"

Tim leaned against the front fender and draped his arms across his chest. He liked how impressed she was; it made him feel warm inside. "I seem to know a lot about women. They fascinate me. Intrigue me, really." He grinned. "Women are much more interesting than men, I think. Way more complex. I don't think they're from Venus, they're from another galaxy."

She erupted in laughter—that lusty low sound that made his loins stir. He drew in a ragged breath. "God, you have a great laugh."

His remark made her laughter stop abruptly, and he was sorry he'd said it. He'd said the same thing fifteen years ago, hadn't he, and gotten a similar reaction. Once again, Tim had entered no-no territory.

"Well, thanks for walking me," Sarah said, not meeting his eyes as she focused her concentration on something inside her purse. After groping around in there for a bit, she came up with a set of car keys.

Yeah, Tim thought. He had most definitely disquieted her.

And, like all those years before, he wasn't ready to—wouldn't, *couldn't,* damn it—stop yet. "That's what attracted me to you back then, that laugh of yours. It sounded so strange, coming from such a skinny, tentative little thing. It was as though a ventriloquist was hidden nearby, laughing for you."

Raising her head, she finally met his gaze. He could see her gathering her poise around her like a cloak. "Yes, well, that thinness was me starving to fit into my wedding dress, which I'd bought two sizes too small on purpose. And as for being tentative, I was. Not only shy, but insecure and terrified and just out of high school. 'Bride's nerves,' they call it."

"A very young bride."

"Too young, yes."

"So, you're older now, and wiser."

After a pause, she said wryly, "It is to be devoutly hoped."

He unfolded his arms and draped one on the hood of her car, then leaned in just a little. Was it his imagination, or did her breath quicken as he did? In the cool, clear night, her faint perfume—old-fashioned tea roses mixed with something lemony—drifted into his nostrils. He inhaled it slowly.

"Now you're old enough to know what you're doing," he said quietly.

"I think so." Her voice cracked a little.

"Think?"

"Know."

"So, your fiancé—what's his name?"

"Charles."

"Charles. He's the right one, I guess."

Sarah swallowed nervously. Oh, how she hated lying, but she couldn't see a way to gracefully extricate herself from this one. Besides, she didn't really have to. She planned never to see Tim again. "Sure," she said, mentally crossing her fingers. "The right one."

Twirling around, she tried to jam her key into the lock, missed, tried again and got it. She opened the door partway, then angled her head to face Tim. His body blocked out most of the illumination from the nearby parking-lot lights, creating the effect of a halo shining around him, around his virile, broad-shouldered outline. Something somersaulted in her stomach area, and she had to swallow down the urge to giggle nervously.

"Well, good night," she managed. "I hope you got something out of the class."

He hesitated for a moment, then said easily, "Oh, yeah, I got something. Drive safely."

He held open the door for her as she got in, then closed it after her. She adjusted her seat belt, started the car, waved briefly, and drove off without a backward glance.

Except for a quick peek in the rearview mirror. Tim stood still as a statue in the empty parking lot, his glowing image fading as her taillights drew farther away.

"Where have you been, Sarah?"

"Lois," Sarah said into the phone, "it's ten-thirty." Juggling the receiver, she took off her earrings and kicked off her shoes, then unzipped her skirt all the way down. "I just walked in. I was teaching tonight."

"Well, I just got in from Cincinnati," Lois drawled in her slow Southern way, "by way of Atlanta, Boulder and Fargo, North Dakota, and I'm about to sleep for three years.'' Lois was a flight attendant for an airline that was noted for short hops. ''Thanks for feeding Killer.''

''That is still the stupidest name for a sweet little kitty cat I have ever heard.'' Lifting her hips, Sarah rolled down her panty hose, gave a sigh of relief and settled into her favorite living-room chair. Kicking the hose off, she put her feet up on a nearby hassock and sighed once again. She hated feeling bound up by her clothes.

''The name's Killer so he'll get a little more aggressive. Poor thing's too timid by half.'' Lois let out a long yawn. ''Oo-ee! Sorry. So, anything I should know about before I hibernate?''

''Well, I ran into—I can't say an old friend because I barely knew him, but a guy I used to go to school with, back at San Francisco State. Fifteen years ago. He manages a radio station, KCAW.''

''Single?''

''Yes.''

''Straight?''

''Decidedly.''

''You want him?''

''Nope.''

''Can I have him?''

Sarah chuckled. ''Lo, you haven't even met him. You know nothing about him.''

''Honey, when you've been without as long as I have, and you hear about a single guy with a steady job and some college, he sounds like heaven. Is he nice looking?''

''I guess so.''

''Funny? Tall?''

''Yes, funny, and tall enough.''

''So?'' Lois let the word linger for a little bit. ''What's the drawback?''

''Nothing, if you want to have fun. But he's not for the long term. Don't get your heart involved.''

"It's my other organs that need some male-type company, thank you. My heart gets on all by itself."

"You have no shame," Sarah said with a grin.

"Well, I certainly hope I don't. What's his name?"

"Tim. Tim Pelham." Sarah rubbed the pads of her fingertips over her eyes. The high from teaching was now gone, and weariness had taken its place.

"Tim. Nice, unpretentious guy name. Well listen, I'm about to fall asleep on my feet. Keep this Tim around for when I wake up, 'kay? Hey, sure you don't want him? He sounds yummy."

"Nope. I'm on a diet. For a change."


Tim popped open another can of beer and stared into the fireplace. His condo's den was warm and wood-paneled, with a view of downtown San Francisco that could serve as a picture postcard. But he noticed nothing except the way the flames worked on the log, gnawing away at the sides, gradually edging toward the middle.

Going back to the station hadn't done the trick, and after a couple of hours there, he'd left. Maybe he should have gone to Sully's, after all. He was restless, needing a little company.

But the company he wanted was unavailable. Reaching into his pocket, he withdrew a few calling cards from this evening, looked at them, then tore them up and put them in the ashtray next to the sofa he was slumped on.

He should be feeling down about Gail, but what he was feeling was relief that he didn't have to deal with her anymore. He should be sleeping, but he was too on edge. He shouldn't be having a second beer, but hey, what the hell?

Didn't take a genius to figure out the problem. He couldn't get Sarah out of his mind. And every time he thought of her, he felt a surge of pressure between his legs. It was as though he'd had a hard-on for fifteen years and had just became aware of it. That was the only explanation he had for this...fixation about her. She wouldn't leave him alone.

Timing. Sometimes it sucked.

He took a sip of his beer and let the cold, crisp taste slide down his throat. Yeah, timing. Back then, all those years ago, the timing had been off. And tonight, it was still off. Even if she weren't engaged to someone else, she'd slammed the door in his face quite emphatically, then double-locked it.

Best thing to do, and he knew it, was to put Sarah Dann out of his mind. Nodding slowly, he took another slug of beer. Yes, best thing to do. Absolutely the best thing.

Right.

# 4

"Marianne," Sarah called out, marking off her Projects list with a yellow highlighter. "Has the printer sent the proofs for the Christmas bulletin yet?"

"Nope," came her secretary's reply from the outer office.

"Again? Why are they always late? Get them on the phone for me, will you?"

"Will do."

"And have we got the signed contract from Ravi Dhuran for the January schedule? He pulls in about five hundred people, but he's flaked out before, so I'm not going to put his class in until I have a firm commitment."

"Yeah, got it, it's...somewhere here, on my desk."

"Well, how about bringing it somewhere here, to my desk? And is the coffee coffee yet?"

Sarah's secretary/assistant Marianne appeared in the doorway. She was in her late forties, had short curly silver hair, an athletic body, and was not in the least cowed by her employer. She set down a steaming cup of coffee in front of Sarah and lifted an eyebrow. "What's going on, boss lady? Tummy upset? Got up on the wrong side of bed this morning? I would ask about PMS but you'd probably bite my head off."

Sarah removed her reading glasses and set them down

on a pile of documents. "Marianne, is this your way of saying I'm being a little grumpy?"

"Bingo. And not just a little."

Sarah frowned, then rubbed her eyelids, realizing too late that she was creating dark mascara smudges under her eyes. "Terrific move," she muttered to herself, then glared at Marianne. "Okay, I'm a grump. Aren't I allowed moods? Everyone else around here is allowed moods."

"You sure are," Marianne soothed.

"I mean it's not like I yelled at you or anything." She tunneled her fingers through her hair before remembering she'd pinned it back in a severe bun this morning. It was no longer severe, nor was it a bun. Scratch one more hairdo. Sighing, she began pulling several large hairpins out, dropping them into a porcelain dish on her desk.

She smiled ruefully at Marianne. "I'm such a mess. I really needed a good sleep last night and really didn't get it. I function on eight hours, can make do with six, but two or three—I'm barely conscious." Pulling a couple of tissues out of a dispenser, she wet one with her tongue, then rubbed under her eyes. "If I snapped your head off, I'm sorry."

"Wanna talk about it?"

"Nothing to talk about. It was just one of those awful, endless nights where your mind is not aware it is supposed to be resting."

"Well, I have some stuff I got at the health-food store, if you're interested—"

At that moment, a knock on the outer door made both women look at each other. No one who worked at Keep On Learning ever knocked.

"Expecting anyone?" Marianne asked.

"Nope."

Marianne turned around, partially closed her employer's door and spoke to someone out of Sarah's sight. "May I help you?'' Sarah heard her say in her best business manner.

''I'm looking for Sarah Dann.''

A small zap of panic hit her at the sound of the man's voice, and she clutched the edge of her desk. Him? Again? Really, hadn't she been clear enough? Hadn't he listened? He was to leave her alone.

''Do you have an appointment?'' Marianne asked.

''Nope.''

''May I ask what this is in reference to?''

''Um, yeah, you can ask—'' Sarah imagined the slow, easy grin on his face ''—but I'm not sure I could tell you. All right, I think I need to see her about a class.''

''One you want to take or have already taken?''

''Both, actually.''

''May I be of help? Or we have several assistants who handle sign-ups—''

''Nope,'' he interrupted cheerfully. ''I need to see the boss.''

''Oh. Your name, please?''

''Tim Pelham.''

''I'll check to see if Ms. Dann is available.''

Marianne came back into Sarah's office, closing the door behind her and leaning against it in an exaggerated pose of maidenly wonder. ''There is a very nice-looking man out there. I mean, *really* nice looking. Tim Pelham. Know him?''

Sarah found a mirror in her desk drawer and peered into it. She groaned. ''Yes, I know him.'' She rubbed some more under her eyes, then tried to fluff up her hair so that it appeared wild and free by design. ''Tell him I can't see anyone now, okay? That I'm busy, I'm on the phone, in the middle of a meeting.''

She put the mirror down and massaged her temples.

Coward, she thought. "No, don't say any of that. Oh, heck, give me two minutes, then send Mr. Charm right in."

Tim noted the expression on Sarah's face the moment he entered her office—mostly wariness, but he thought there was a little flustered pleasure thrown in. He immediately decided to take it slow and easy until she stopped looking at him as though he had a reputation for selling bridges.

She was on the phone and signaled him to take a seat.

"Yes, Sid," she said. "Well, I've had nothing but wonderful responses. We hope you'll offer another seminar for us, maybe the beginning of next year?...Oh?...I see. Well, call me when you get into town. See you."

After hanging up, she looked over at him.

Tim was still standing. "Hi there," he said.

Sarah nodded, then lowered her eyes to a pile of paperwork on her desk. "Hello. What can I do for you?"

Ice, impersonal ice—that was her tack this morning, Tim thought. Not rolling out the hospitality wagon. Okay, so he was an idiot for showing up. But he was here because he *had* to see her again, that was all. Engaged or not, cold or not, suspicious or not, he wanted to be with her, one more time, to—

What? Make sure last night wasn't a dream? That she didn't affect him as strongly as he remembered, both fifteen years ago and sitting in her class twelve hours earlier?

Her glorious, vibrant hair fanned out from her face like a messy cloud, there were dark shadows under her eyes and she was currently trying to chew off what was left of her lipstick. But the sight of her still got him right in the gut, and lower; still warmed his blood and made breathing more difficult.

What was it about Sarah Dann? He'd known women more beautiful, with better bodies, women who made him feel welcomed instead of something that might bring on an allergic reaction. But, there was no logic here. None whatsoever. He was here...because he was here.

Easing himself into a comfortable leather chair, Tim gazed around the room. One whole wall was lined with bookcases, filled with hundreds of books on subjects such as dieting, eliminating clutter, healing, foreclosures for financial prosperity, meditation, adoption, reincarnation, leadership, and over twenty phone books.

The cream-colored walls were hung with seascapes and paintings of flowers; also a huge bulletin board packed with notes and a large calendar with red and green lines through various dates. The furniture was non-fussy wood, there were dried flowers in vases and several clay pots with real plants perched on the windowsill.

His eye paused on two instruments that looked like clarinets or recorders hung over her door in the shape of an X. There was also a full tree in the corner with a red ribbon tied around it, and both a large crystal suspended from a slender thread and brass wind chimes hung in front of the window.

The whole thing was pleasantly crowded, not compulsively neat, and not overly decorated. Warm, personal. "Nice office," he said.

"Thank you."

"What's that over the door?"

"They're ancient flutes. They're supposed to keep the spirits away. It's part of the Fêng shui tradition."

"Fêng shui?"

"Back about four years ago, we had someone come in and train us. It's an ancient Chinese system of bringing order and peace to a place of work. The tree and the ribbon represent money and success, the crystal, enlightenment, and so on. It's too complicated to explain it all now."

"Do you believe in this stuff?"

"I don't know. Some of my employees believe with heart and soul." She shrugged. "I figure it can't hurt."

She lifted a pair of glasses from the desk and put them on. He could barely see her eyes behind the thick lenses.

"You didn't wear those last night."

"Correct. I wore contact lenses. So, what brings you here so nice and early—" she looked at her watch pointedly "—at nine o'clock?"

He propped an ankle on the opposite knee. Her desk held a computer terminal, was piled with stacks of papers and framed at each end with a Rollodex. This was one very busy lady.

"Well, I got to thinking," he said. "I used to teach a little—you know, recording technique, how to break into radio, news versus entertainment, stuff like that. What do you say?"

"About what?"

"About me teaching a class here, at your school."

Folding her hands in front of her on her desk, she took a moment to consider, but he knew her answer before she stated it crisply. "Thanks for the offer, Tim, but we're pretty well covered in media classes. So—"

He was being dismissed. But he wasn't about to take the hint. "All right, then, what else can I offer?"

"Offer? What do you mean?"

"In return for your services."

"My services?"

"Yeah, you know, for my love life." He was inventing as fast as he could; somehow, the words kept coming.

"Your love life?"

"Sure. I did take your class, didn't I? I've been thinking. It's time to, well, get serious. Maybe settle down." That one just popped out, but it was just the thing to get her attention; he knew it the minute he'd said it. "Like I told you," he continued with a small smile, "I don't seem to meet the 'forever' kind of woman, so I thought you could, you know, help me. Be my personal consultant."

"Your personal consultant."

Sarah admonished herself to stop repeating everything Tim said, but her head was fogging up and she couldn't seem to concentrate on much. Something about this man, about being in his presence, threw her totally off-balance.

She took off her glasses and set them down. Without the blurring effect of the reading lenses, she was able to meet his gaze full on, making contact for the first time with those dreamy, sky blue eyes of his. She knew immediately, from the way her heart fluttered, that she should have kept the glasses on.

"Yeah," Tim said with a grin. "I'm new at this. Dating with a purpose, I mean. Help me fill out my list of Must Haves and Deal Breakers, maybe recommend some women—you probably know a whole bunch of the right kind...your friends, or women who take classes here."

An overweight, balding young man came hurrying into the office. "We've been brainstorming on the Net thing," he announced to Sarah, "and we've come up with a terrific magazine idea for the web page. Listen to this—"

"Ira," Sarah said, "write it up, and we'll talk about it at the two o'clock meeting."

"But I thought you'd want—"

She seemed more amused than put off by the intrusion. "I'm busy right now."

Ira looked startled, then noticed Tim for the first time. "Oh. Okay, talk to you later," he told Sarah, then rushed out as quickly as he'd rushed in.

"I have an open-door policy," she explained. "So, you were saying you want to hire me."

"I guess I am. Are you for hire?"

Sarah allowed herself to lean back in her desk chair, ordering her shoulders to stop hunching up in defense against whatever it was Tim Pelham's presence aroused in her. Pure hormones, she figured. She needed to stop reading romance novels before she went to sleep.

Or maybe she was ovulating and Mother Nature was putting out a general call for sperm donors.

"To be honest," she said, "I've never done anything like that before—I mean on a one-on-one basis. The follow-up matchmaking is handled by one of my assistants. Not that I couldn't," she added quickly. "I'm sure I could, that is, if I had the time, which I really don't—"

He interrupted her. "How much would you charge? for your personal services, I mean."

"I have no idea. I'm not sure what it would entail."

The intercom buzzed, for which Sarah was grateful. She needed to regroup here, gather her thoughts. "Yes, Marianne?" she replied.

"Damon Frontera from New York, about Thomas Bernstein."

"I have to take this," Sarah said to Tim, then spoke into the receiver. "Damon, so glad you could call me back...."

While Sarah took care of her business call, Tim grabbed a blank pad from her desk and jotted down some quick notes off the top of his head. By the time she'd hung up, he could see that she'd decided not to entertain the thought of being his consultant, and was, indeed, about to tell him to take a hike, so he offered his pad to her and smiled. "I started already. There're a few Must Haves I thought of."

She began to say something, seemed to change her mind, then glanced down at his list. "Sports nut?"

"Absolutely. I spend a lot of time at ball games—football, basketball, baseball, even hockey—and in front of the TV when I'm not at the game. I wouldn't want one of those women who say, 'Oh? Another game? Isn't it over yet?' You know the type."

Sarah actually smiled for an instant. "I sure do. I'm one of them."

*Damn*, he thought. What a shame.

The door flew open. "Sarah," said a female who looked barely seventeen, dressed in a T-shirt and jeans and carrying a clipboard. "What about making your own perfume? Madge met a lady at Esalen last weekend who's into it. Knows all about it."

"Hmm. Did Madge get her card?"

"Yeah. Got it right here." She patted the clipboard.

"That sounds interesting, Shadow. Write up a proposal on it, okay?"

Shadow seemed very pleased. "Yeah. All right. Thanks."

She went out, slamming the door behind her. It was obvious she'd been totally unaware of Tim's presence.

"Sorry, again," Sarah said, glancing once more at Tim's list. "'Not too skinny, not too fat,'" she read. "How about age?"

"I don't know.... Twenty-five to forty?"

"How old are you?"

"Thirty eight." Grinning, he patted the top of his head. "I look older with the silver stuff, huh? One of my friends does that comb-in dye stuff. Says I ought to try it."

"No, don't," she said, obviously horrified. Then she added, more impersonally, "I'm sorry, it's none of my business. I just think a little silver in a man's hair is very attractive."

In a *man's* hair, she'd said, not in *your* hair. But it was something, anyway, he thought.

Crumbs.

Well, yeah, maybe crumbs, but her interest was piqued by the challenge he'd offered her, he could tell.

Hey, what the hell. Maybe she had some doubts about her upcoming marriage, or had just as much of a need to settle the old itch as he did and was fighting it. He needed to play this one out, wherever it led.

"'Pleasant voice,'" Sarah read, then looked up at him.

He shrugged. "Can't stand nags or women with high-pitched, screechy voices."

"Neither can I. All right." She set the pad down and rested her clasped hands on top of it. "What else? What *must* you have in a woman?"

"You have the time?" He sat straighter in his chair. She was going for it. "I mean, now?"

She glanced at her watch. "I'll give you another five minutes, so we can see if there's anything here to work with."

"Fair enough. Must Haves... I guess your basic good talk, great sex, and lots of laughs. What else is there?"

"Do you like artistic women? Down-to-earth and practical? Motherly, childish? Neat? Affectionate, removed, intellectual?"

"Sure."

"Which?"

"Any of 'em. I told you, so far I haven't been choosing any keepers, so I'm willing to try a large assortment of types."

Sarah nodded and made a couple of notes on the pad. "Next—Will Settle."

He frowned. "Can't think of anything offhand. Two years each way added on to the age range?"

"How about religion?"

"Not important as long as she's not a fanatical anything. Also I don't care much about hair color or height. Don't even care about beauty, as long as she's decent looking and likes herself. Sound okay?"

"Downright open-minded of you," Sarah said wryly.

He spread his hands. "Hey, that's the kind of guy I am.

I told you, I like women. I find them fascinating." He chuckled and after a moment, almost reluctantly, so did she.

Then their gazes locked; the smile left both their faces instantly. Tim felt his breath catch. No way could he miss that quick dart of awareness in her eyes—it probably matched the one in his—so he repeated softly, "Fascinating."

Sarah's throat constricted, and she coughed to dispel the momentary intimacy that had sizzled between them like a flame racing along a dynamite fuse. *Get him out of here,* an inner voice warned, even as she heard herself saying calmly, "All right. Let's hear your Deal Breakers."

He scratched his head. "Jeez, I don't know. Oh, yeah. Nothing too—you know—far-out in the bed department."

"Pardon?"

"I'm not into pain or sadism or cross-dressing. Fine for others, but I'm pretty straight-arrow that way."

Her throat closed up again at the thought of "straight-arrow" sex with Tim Pelham, but—again—she swallowed down the sudden obstruction. Donning her glasses, she made a notation: "Likes his sex straight." As she stared at the words she had to bite back the swift urge to giggle nervously, just as she had the night before.

The door was flung open and Tara strode in, all red-haired, miniskirted, six feet two inches of her. With a hand perched on her hip, she asked, "Do we have to do another infant-care class? We didn't have enough numbers the last time, and aren't we getting just a little bit sick of the whole natural-childbirth breast-feeding mother-and-child-bonding crap?"

*Rescued,* Sarah thought, and, removing her glasses, smiled. "You may be sick of it, Tara, but the world just keeps on procreating, so, sorry. It stays in."

"But, Sarah—"

"I have company, Tara. Meet Tim Pelham."

Tara swerved around and when she saw him, her eyes traveled up and down his body, then up again. "Well," she said, with a raised eyebrow. "Hello."

He nodded. "Hi."

Tara turned back to Sarah, said, "Talk to you later," and left the office with an exaggerated swing of her hips.

Tim's gaze followed her out the door, his mouth hanging open.

"She your type?" Sarah couldn't resist saying.

"Are you kidding? She's terrifying."

"Her husband doesn't think so. And he's about five-six. They're madly in love."

"You're serious."

"Scout's honor. But she did remind me of something. Do you want children?"

"Someday, yeah."

She nodded. "I must say, you don't have any real barriers set up. It should be easy to find a lot of candidates."

The intercom buzzed again, and Sarah pressed the button. "Marianne, I'm tied up here for a few more minutes. Take a message and tell everyone else not to come in for a little bit."

"Gotcha."

"You mean that?" Tim asked. "I'm easy? Then why haven't I found my dream woman?"

Loaded question, Sarah thought. Picking up her glasses, she sat back in her chair and chewed on the end of one earpiece. "It's possible you don't really want her."

"What do you mean?"

No, she thought. Don't start getting into motivation and psychology. She waved a hand in the air vaguely. "Nothing. Or, rather, I don't know you well enough to talk about this. I'm sorry." She pushed herself up from her desk chair. "Well, it's about that time...."

Tim remained seated. "Really, tell me."

"No," she said firmly. "Your private life is truly none of my business." She came around the desk and walked to the door, hoping he would take the rather broad hint. With her hand on the knob, she turned to face him. "We'll have to do this another time."

Tim still remained seated, swiveling his chair around to face her. Leaning forward, he rested his elbows on his knees, his hands dangling loosely between his legs. "Don't you like me, Sarah?" he asked quietly. "I like you."

His sincerity threw her; had she hurt his feelings? Guilt washed over her. "Of course, I like you," she said truthfully. "You're fun. And, I think, kind. So then, yes, I like you. And so will several women I can think of."

"Several?" He sat up straighter.

"Several."

"And I'm easy?"

"You sure are."

Tim got up slowly and walked toward her with an amused grin. "Compared to what?"

Flustered, she found herself taking a step backward. "Most people have more obvious likes and dislikes."

"Do you?"

"Yes, I suppose I do."

Now he stood right in front of her, and her pulse picked up speed.

"Tell me about your list," he said.

"My list?"

"You know—Must Haves, Deal Breakers, et cetera."

He was so close; she got a whiff of aftershave that suggested a fresh, sailing-on-the-ocean-in-the-sunshine kind of day. Her hand found its way to her throat, and she clutched the small emerald that dangled there from a gold chain, holding on for dear life. "This is not about me, it's about you."

His eyes roamed over her face; even through her astigmatism, she sensed his movements as though they were a heat lamp. "I need an idea why I'm so easy," he said. "Maybe I'm missing something. What's your number-one Must Have?"

She took another step back, walked around him and headed for her office window. It looked out on the parking lot, but it was a nice parking lot, filled with trees and bushes and flowers; the view usually calmed her down.

Keeping her back to Tim, Sarah said, "I don't know about number one, but I want kids, so he has to. I love ballet and classical music, and the ocean, so it would be nice if he did, too. I don't care for sports. And he has to be someone without a weight fixation. I've been going up and down twenty pounds my whole life and I'm probably not about to change. That's about it. Okay?"

"Where are you now in your twenty pounds?"

"Not where I want to be," she said wryly.

There was a moment of silence, then she heard him approaching. "I think you're perfect just as you are."

Her hands flew to her flushed cheeks. She'd always wanted to hear those words—the acceptance behind them that, flaws and all, she was worth it.

He was right behind her now. Steeling herself, she wheeled around to face him. "If you're for real, you're too good to be true."

Grinning, he asked, "Is 'too good to be true' on your list?"

"It is not."

"Then tell me more, please."

She threw her hands up. "Why?"

"It's helpful, really it is."

Again, she retreated by walking over to the painting on the wall behind her desk, one of her favorites—a small child playing with shells at the seashore. Why was she allowing Tim to take up her time this way?

And why wasn't she fighting very hard?

"All right," she said, turning to face him.

He remained at the window. The hanging crystal caught a shaft of sunlight, and rainbow prisms glinted all around him.

"A couple more things from my list," she said, "and then I have to get back to work."

"So do I."

"Good." She gripped the back of her desk chair. "Age-wise, he should be, well, reasonable," she said briskly. "From ten years younger to ten years older, so we have some frame of reference, I guess. And tall enough so I don't feel silly in heels. But that's not absolutely necessary. And I don't want a man who's searching for his identity or who doesn't know what he wants to be when he grows up. I want him already grown-up, someone who knows who he is."

She took a deep breath and expelled it. "There. That about does it."

"I assume Charles has all these qualities."

"Who? Charles?" Whoops, Sarah thought. Almost got her there. "Yes, he does. So, no more about me. If I agree to this—to finding you some available, attractive women who want to get married—"

"Wait a minute." He held up a hand. "I didn't say married. I'm not ready to actually get married yet. I'd just like the next step from where I am now."

She crossed her arms. "And where would that be?"

"Where I am now..." He perched on the edge of her desk and scratched his head. "There's been an emptiness lately. A sense that there ought to be more to being with a woman than what I usually feel. I don't know. This is not something I've put into words."

"You're doing fine. Except you don't like the word *marriage*. Any particular reason?"

"Gee, I don't know."

"I don't mean to pry—"

"No, no, you're not, but I haven't talked about this with anyone. I guess it's something about an aversion to feeling tied down. Terrified is more like it—of losing my freedom."

Freedom to do what? Sarah wanted to ask, but didn't because she didn't need to. Tim Pelham fit the Peter Pan theory to a T. Great at playing, terror of commitment....

And utterly irresistible.

*Enough*, she counseled herself silently. Get back to work and get the man out of your office and back to his job.

His job. The radio station. Radio.

It was light-bulb time.

Yes, of course, Sarah thought with a mental snap of her fingers. It was perfect.

"You know, Tim," she said, immediately energized as she came around to the front of her desk. "I think this will work out. In fact, I'm sure it will."

Tim was surprised by Sarah's sudden enthusiasm, but pleased. "Good. Name your price."

She smiled at him now, obviously much more at ease. What in the world had happened, he wondered, all of a sudden?

"How do you feel about barter?" she asked.

"Pardon?"

"Trading services for services. I need advertising for the school. On your radio station. It would be a great boost for us. I've relied on print ads so far because broadcast is so expensive."

"Ah."

"The school does pretty well, but my dream is to get all those classrooms filled. Radio ads are just the ticket."

He nodded slowly as he thought it over. It could be done,

easily. "Sure. We can record some fifteen-second spots to run once in a while—"

"Good."

"And I can even get you on one of our talk shows as a guest."

"Even better," Sarah said with a huge grin. "So, do we have a deal?" She offered her hand.

He took it, gave her a firm handshake, then held on to it a little longer than necessary. He liked the softness of her skin, he liked the smell of her, the smattering of freckles on her nose. Hell, he just liked being close to her. "We have a deal."

"Airtime—" Sarah extricated her hand from his and propped it on her hip "—in exchange for me giving you personal, hands-on help with finding the woman of your dreams."

He'd already found a bunch of those, Tim thought, but didn't say it out loud. He figured she was talking about a different kind of dream woman. The kind with *substance*.

And maybe that was why he was here today. Maybe it really was time to rethink his taste in women, stop going for the beautiful package and look more thoroughly beneath the wrapping. With a mental shrug, he thought it was worth a shot.

And this way, he could keep close, personal contact with Sarah.

5

Apparently, close personal contact was not quite what Sarah had in mind. Phoning Tim at work the next morning, she informed him everything would be handled by faxes and telephone, that in-person consultations would interfere too much with her very busy schedule. She messengered over photographs and all pertinent information on five women; should he choose to call one of them, she told him, it would be all right for him to say that Sarah suggested it.

He, in turn, told her he would get some copy written for her ads, fax them to her for approval, then have his station announcer record them. It was all very businesslike, very matter-of-fact.

And Tim felt as let down as a balloon the morning after a birthday party.

He wasn't sure what he'd expected, but it seemed as though Sarah had decided to avoid seeing him again. That knowledge created a hollow feeling in his gut, and he sure didn't care for the sensation. He tried to look at the facts: Sarah was a very busy person, with a business to run and, even now, was probably planning a wedding.

Planning a wedding.

That last one drove him to Sully's for a beer at lunchtime. Sitting on his favorite stool at the long wooden bar, and idly checking out the previous evening's sports highlights on ESPN, he considered the situation once again.

*Take the hint, Pelham,* was what he kept coming up with. Sarah Dann was engaged and unavailable. Sure, she was as attracted to him as he was to her. But she was being a grown-up, ignoring the surge of sexuality between them the way grown-ups often had to. Life didn't always allow you to get what you wanted.

He, on the other hand, was acting like a randy kid with fire in his pants who wanted gratification, and wanted it now, without a care in the world for consequences. Not a pleasant picture.

Tim's fist hit the counter with resolve, making Sully glance at him with a lifted eyebrow. Tim smiled at his longtime friend and shook his head, signaling to pay him no attention, everything was okay. Which it was.

He, too, could be a grown-up, by God. Sarah was out of the picture. He would call up those five women. He would meet them. He would try, really try to find the special one for him.

Even though he wasn't quite sure he believed in the concept.

Which called for another beer.


Sarah pressed the intercom button. "Marianne? Do I have lunch or drinks with Judy Littner-Kragan tomorrow?"

"Drinks. At five."

"I wonder what she's like in person? Have you seen her on talk shows?"

"Nope. She doesn't do them, says it interferes with her writing muse."

"And she has a bestseller anyway—what a gal."

Seconds later, Marianne spoke over the intercom. "Tim Pelham for you."

She picked up the receiver. "Sarah Dann."

"Were you aware that Bethany Thomas has had a makeover since she was in your class two years ago?"

"Pardon?"

"Did you know that your, quote, down-to-earth computer expert who loves to cook and spend quiet evenings in front of the fire, unquote, now has a very large tattoo on her left wrist that says Goddess, with a snake coiled around it?"

Sarah's eyes widened. "You're kidding."

"Nope. She apparently has a lot more tattoos, offered to show them to me right at the restaurant. I turned her down."

"Oh, dear."

"And her hair, which in her picture was pale blond, is now purple."

Sarah bit her bottom lip to keep from laughing out loud, but the giggle erupted anyway. "You are kidding, right?"

"And it sticks up in spikes. In fact, I was afraid if I touched it, I'd slice my fingers off."

She gave in finally and out came peals and peals of merriment at the picture Tim painted, until she was gasping for breath.

Marianne threw open the door and mouthed, "Are you all right?" Wiping at the tears of laughter, Sarah nodded and waved her out of the office.

Tim listened with a smile on his face. That husky, low chuckle that had gotten to him all those years ago totally disappeared in Sarah's full-blown belly laugh, and he felt pleased with himself for bringing it out.

"Anyway," he said as she seemed to be settling down, "thanks a whole bunch."

"But, didn't you call her before you met? Talk to her on the phone?"

"Sure." He pushed back his desk chair and tilted it so it was resting on the wall behind him. Then he put his feet up on his desk; he was now in his favorite schmoozing position. "And yeah, she sounded a little offbeat. But I figured if she had that Keep On Learning seal of approval, how bad could she be?''

"Oh, Tim, I'm so sorry. I had no idea—''

"Not your fault,'' he interrupted her quickly. "Actually, it was pretty amusing after a while. I got a kick out of watching the other people in the restaurant checking her out.''

"At least you found something of interest.''

"Sure. But there will be no follow-up contact, I assure you.''

Sarah sighed. "Poor Bethany. And poor you. I hope she hasn't soured you on the whole list.''

"Nope. I'm still in there plugging away.''

"Attaboy.''

"I keep thinking it used to be easier than this, but then I remember the dry mouth and the fear of rejection when I used to ask girls out.''

"You? Afraid of rejection?''

"Why do you sound so surprised?''

"I'm sorry, I just… I don't know, you seem so sure of yourself, so comfortable.''

"I suppose I am. Now. But back then?'' He chuckled, remembering. "Man, I was a basket case. Her name was Jane. Jane O'Hanlon, and I asked her to go for a walk and an ice-cream cone. My knees were shaking so hard, I thought I'd take a header right there on the sidewalk and make an ass of myself.''

"You poor thing.'' She sounded genuinely compassionate. "How old were you?''

"Eleven, I think.''

"Eleven? That doesn't count. I mean, you weren't dating at eleven. You were, I don't know, socializing, maybe. You weren't even a teenager yet.''

"I was already shaving and had several chest hairs, which I counted every morning. And I called it a date. I was male, she was female. I was powerfully attracted to her and wanted to be with her. She was fourteen, I think, and laughed in my face.''

"Oh, how terrible. I mean, it could have scarred you for life.''

"Could have. It didn't. Just made me want her even more. I asked her again the following year. I had even more chest hair then. She said yes.''

"Yes to what?''

"Do you really want to know?''

"Actually, no, I don't. Were your parents aware, I mean, about your interest in girls?''

"Parent. Singular. My mother ran off when I was two. And my old man enjoyed his bottle, so he wasn't conscious enough most of the time to know what I was doing. I guess I was a little on the precocious side, but I got through it without any major tragedies. Plain luck, I guess.'' Balancing the phone between his shoulder and ear, he tossed a paperweight in the shape of a baseball back and forth between his palms. He was enjoying this conversation a lot.

"So, anything else you want to know about me?'' he asked. "Fire away. I have very few secrets.''

Sarah found herself unexpectedly moved by Tim's revelation. Not only abandoned by his mother, but left with an alcoholic father who showed very little interest. What an awful childhood to have to go through. Had there been other family? Aunts, uncles? Someone to care about him? Anyone to love him?

The question was on the tip of her tongue, but even though the two of them were chatting away like old buddies, she didn't think it wise to push for any more personal information. Something about that smacked of an intimacy she didn't want to encourage.

"Maybe another time,'' she said. "I have a bunch of work on my desk.''

"Yeah. Me, too. Okay. Wish me luck with number two."

"Oh, yes, the list. Who's the lucky girl?"

"Lisa-Marie Phelps."

"I don't remember right offhand—"

"Psychologist? Works with teenagers." Tim picked up the information sheet and read, "Running enthusiast, collects antiques, divorced, no kids, five-two, thirty-one."

"How long ago did she take the class?"

"Last year."

"Let's hope she hasn't had some kind of life-altering experience since then. And Tim, thanks for being a good sport. Not a lot of people would be able to keep their sense of humor."

"Hey, if you can't laugh you cry, right?"

"Right. Bye."

Sarah replaced her receiver and sat for a moment, a twinge of sadness in her throat for the little boy who had been Tim Pelham. He hadn't seemed troubled when he'd told her about it, though, so maybe her sympathy was misplaced.

Ignoring the files and lists of phone calls to be returned on her desk, she stared at the wind chimes while she played back the rest of their conversation. Purple hair. Tattoos. Poor man.

She grinned. In no time, she found herself laughing again.

"And I find that if I concentrate real hard, and block out all other stimuli, I can get back to a prenatal memory, of being tossed and turned back and forth in the warm liquid, of having no real anchor except for the umbilicus, and that, too, is weaving and always in motion. That sense of rootlessness, of being heaved left and right and up and down by the fates, with no one coming to my rescue—it's what has stayed with me all these years. It's been responsible for my lack of commitment to anything or anyone, for my suspicions of both men and women, why I didn't really have any close friends or lasting love relationships.''

''I see.'' Tim nodded for what was probably the sixtieth time, wondering if his drooping upper lids were too obvious.

''But with this inner-child growth work—not that stuff on the bestseller list,'' Lisa-Marie added with parenthetical disdain, ''but Dr. Marculopolos's womb-box, all the exercises, plus that saline and herb water to re-create gestation—I'm gradually changing that kind of behavior.''

She grabbed a quick sip of coffee, but before Tim was able to put in a word, went right on, her whispery, low-pitched voice at odds with her intensity. ''Do you see? By having the key to parenting myself properly, I can be the parent of my own child and trust myself not to make him or her as lost as I was.''

''Well, good for you. Do you ever smile?''

''Huh?''

''Never mind.''

Placing her hand on his and hunching over even more so that she was at eye level with his chest, she said earnestly, ''That's why I was really glad when you called. I've been deep into the ninth level and now I know I'm ready for the tenth.''

''The tenth.''

''Yes. I'm honored to have come this far.''

''How many levels are there?''

''No one knows. Dr. Marculopolos has reached eighteen, but he's sure there're more. I may be going to Athens next summer to work with him.''

''Sounds promising.'' Tim signaled the waiter for the check.

''Not that my whole life is therapy,'' she said, her posture relaxing suddenly as she sat straight up. "I don't want you to think that...."

"No, of course not."

"I counsel my kids and go on my little antiquing weekends in my old car."

"Sounds like fun."

She propped her chin on her hand. "So, tell me about you."

"What do you want to know?"

"Have you ever been in therapy?"

Sarah turned off the hair dryer and picked up the bathroom phone. "Hello?"

"You can call me whatever you like, just don't call me baby."

"Excuse me?"

"This is Tim. Last night I got to be with the most *serious* person I have ever come in contact with. Just being in the room with her made me long to be at a funeral instead."

Sarah propped a hip against her bathroom counter and tried to keep a smile out of her voice. "Hold it. How did you get my number? I'm unlisted."

"Piece of cake—news stations have sources."

"Silly me. So, Lisa-Marie Phelps has joined Bethany in the one-date wonder list. Honestly, she seemed okay."

"She's okay, I'm okay, and you're okay. Except when we're not, I guess. Did you know that you can go into a thing called a womb-box?"

"Pardon?"

"And there are levels upon levels, no one knows how many? And that Lisa-Marie is so into this womb-box stuff, that she could talk of nothing else? For three solid hours?"

"Three hours? Where were you for all that time?"

"I got smart this time. Coffee only, I thought. A short,

quick, let's-take-a-look meeting at Starbuck's. And three hours later—''

She bit back another smile. ''You poor man.''

''Finally I fiddled with my beeper and made it go off, so I'd have an excuse to get away.''

''How—or why—did you last that long?''

''I didn't want to be rude. I mean, the poor woman has enough fear of rejection, I didn't want her to slit her wrists just because I would have preferred to be at a CPA convention than there with her.''

''I don't know what to say.'' The laughter bubbled up, but she put her hand over her mouth to prevent its becoming audible. ''It's so horrible, it's funny. But I really do feel awful.''

''Yeah, I thought about blaming you, but I've decided to be noble instead. Who knows about people? I mean, really knows, from information on a piece of paper?''

''Well, you're being very nice. I'll set you up with another list of five, on the house.''

''I'm not sure. This one might finish me off.''

She chuckled. She was enjoying this phone call, as she'd enjoyed the one a few days before. She and Tim got along so well on the phone, when there wasn't all that unspoken challenge and sexual undercurrent between them. There was a chance the two of them might wind up friends. She would like that, she decided. He was interesting and he made her laugh.

''By the way, Tim—'' she sat on the broad edge of the tub and leaned back against the wall tiles ''—can I change the subject?''

''Please.''

''I heard the first spot for the school. It's good, very effective. Thanks.''

''You listened? I thought you don't like my station.''

''Oh, I never said that. It's just not, you know....''

"Your kind of thing. Well, I'm glad you heard it. I think this barter system is a good idea, I'm just not too hopeful about meeting women this way."

"Why?"

"There's a kind of self-consciousness to the whole thing. The other way is better. You know, you look at someone, at a party or a ball game or whatever. And then she looks back and there's this kind of buzz between you. So you go up and start chatting, or she does, and you go from there. But, this is not the same."

"Why, exactly?"

"It's a setup. I mean, you both know why you're there, and there's no time for...spontaneity, for the buzz. It's awkward. And there's something missing—that excitement you get when you already know the person, because then you're looking forward to seeing them again."

"On the other hand," Sarah said, "this way there's mystery. And possibilities."

"But real low odds for success. I already knew I wanted to be with Jane O'Hanlon before I asked her out. And I'm sure you had someone you felt that way about. Your first date—when was it?"

"I'm almost embarrassed to tell you. I hardly looked at a boy until the end of high school."

"You're kidding."

"It's the truth. I was pretty sheltered, and kept very busy with lessons and after-school activities. My folks were real old-school. Their precious daughter wasn't going to be tempted by anything or anyone until they said it was time."

"Didn't you want to rebel?"

"Sometimes. But I didn't have the guts. Or the belief in myself, I guess. It took a long time and a lot of work to turn that around."

"Amazing."

"What?"

"I admire you. That must have been hard, coming from all that...protection, insulation, and then wind up running a business, taking risks, being in charge of an entire operation. That takes a lot of guts."

"Well, what about you? Coming from a background where you practically had to raise yourself? I mean, you were essentially alone, weren't you? And look how well you've done."

"Naw. Mine's different. It's true I didn't have much of a home life, but I always had friends, and became real self-reliant at a young age. I was lucky."

"You became self-reliant, but someone with the exact same background might have wound up on drugs or in jail or who knows what. I think you're just as admirable as you think I am."

"Well, then, let's agree that we're both pretty special."

"Hear, hear."

There was a brief silence, then Tim said quietly, "You know something, Sarah?"

"What?"

"I like you. I mean, as a person."

Her skin flushed with pleasure, but she said lightly, "You mean, as opposed to a plant?"

"Hey, watch it. I was being serious there for a minute."

"Yeah. I guess it took me by surprise. Okay. I like you, too."

"Better."

Another moment of silence followed, one that felt awkward, especially after the easy back-and-forth exchange that had gone on before. Sarah played with the phone cord. "So, who's next?" she asked finally. "On the list?"

"Debvorah Zewitzky. Stockbroker."

"I remember Debvorah, yes. She's quite pretty."

"Seems so."

"Kind of short, though," Sarah added, then frowned,

wondering why that had come out. Some of her best friends were short.

"Well, we can't all be tall," Tim said magnanimously. "Anything else I should know?"

"Well…" She let that trail off. No, she would not say what had popped into her mind. An ungenerous, downright catty thought.

"Is there?" he prompted.

"Actually, Tim, she may be just to your liking. Have a great time."

Sarah hung up the phone. In the mirror, she saw the thoughtful, preoccupied expression on her face. She had averted the intimacy that seemed to hover about them, waiting to pounce. But if there were any more of these phone calls, she wasn't sure she could avoid it much longer.

In the mirror, she also noted that in the time the conversation had taken, her hair had already curled into its favorite impossibly tight waves. She sighed. Now she would have to wet it down and start all over again.

As she began the familiar ritual, she wondered if Tim was or was not a breast man.

Debvorah certainly was short—not even five feet—but she wore what looked to Tim like six-inch heels. And a very tiny skirt. Good legs; not long but shapely. The same pretty face as in her picture—straight dark brown hair that curved under her jawline, nice brown eyes.

And, he couldn't help noticing, the largest pair of mammaries he'd ever seen on a woman—emphasized even more by her otherwise diminutive size and the tight, formfitting sweater that tucked into the very short skirt.

She tottered toward Tim on her heels, and what he felt toward her, more than anything, was sympathy; she was so obviously trying to be alluring, to impress him. He smiled warmly and offered his hand.

* * *

Sarah's house was a small, cozy-looking wood-frame, on a residential street. Rosebushes lined the walkway and a huge oak draped over the narrow front porch. As he knocked on the door, the smell of logs blazing in a fireplace floated past his nostrils.

The porch light came on, then Sarah opened her door, keeping the screen door between them. She wore a long, pale green terry cloth robe tied at the waist, and her hair was pinned up haphazardly on top of her head, much of it escaping its restraints to tumble around her face. Without makeup or her business attire, she seemed younger and softer, closer to the girl he'd met all those years ago.

"Good evening," Tim said, his hands in his pockets.

"Tim?" She seemed surprised to see him. Then, clutching the hardback book she held against her chest, she said dryly, "I would ask how you know where I live, but I assume you have ways."

"Correct. I thought you might like an in-person report on number three. Debvorah, with a *V*. It's not a lot better than the other two."

She gave a half smile. "You have something against top-heavy women?"

"Nope, not really. Well, except for the balance thing. A good strong wind would probably knock her down."

He waited to see if she would invite him in, and when she made no move to do so, lifted an arm and rested his elbow on the door frame. "No, it's the giggle. It's really annoying—the type that starts out okay and winds up sounding like a chimpanzee's mating call. A person can't change the way she laughs, but it's hopeless. I would murder her one night, I know it."

Sarah couldn't help reacting to his humor with a smile. He really did have the most refreshingly relaxed attitude toward most everything. Still, a small wave of guilt washed over her. Three for three, as in disasters. And she'd picked them out personally.

"I feel awful. I really thought one of these women would work out." She unlatched the screen door, even though she had just a moment earlier decided not to invite him in. "Well, I owe you a cup of coffee, at least."

"Glad to oblige." As he passed her, smelling pleasantly of that fresh, outdoorsy aftershave, Tim gazed around her living room and nodded. "Nice place. Cozy. Do you mind that I'm here? Did I get you in the middle of anything?"

"It's all right. I was just reading." She closed the door behind her, then set her book on a nearby shelf, cover down. Why should she advertise her reading habits and that she'd been deeply involved in ancient Wales and a tale of Druids and forbidden love? So deeply, in fact, that when her very twentieth-century doorbell had rung, she'd jumped nearly out of her skin.

"Would you like that cup of coffee?" she asked. "Or some wine?"

"Wine sounds good." Tim sat down on the flowered sofa and, leaning back, closed his eyes and chuckled. "I need it to dull the sound of that laugh. God, it was terrible."

Again, Sarah had an attack of the guilts. Was she—unconsciously, of course—picking women Tim wouldn't like? The question had to be asked. And answered.

But not at this moment.

Pulling the tie of her robe tighter, she went over to the antique sideboard for glasses and a bottle of Chianti.

"That's a great fireplace you have there. Nice brickwork. There's nothing like a good fire," he said. "I could smell it from outside. I don't know, maybe it's me."

"What's you?" She looked up into the mirror on the wall and met Tim's open gaze in the reflection.

"All these women, all these awful dates. Maybe I'm doing something wrong."

Sarah poured the wine. "I doubt it."

"You're the expert. Is there some kind of secret to this dating thing?"

Holding both glasses, she turned around and walked toward him. "From what you've told me, you're more of an expert than I am. But, I guess the secret is to accept that it's hard work. If you want it badly enough, you go through some discomfort. It gets easier." She set the glasses on the coffee table.

"You ever gone through it? I mean, recently?"

"I sure did. When I was researching the class, I did a thorough study of the whole dating scene for a year."

She settled into the comfortable reading chair adjacent to the couch, but on the opposite end from where Tim sat. On the phone, they'd laughed and bantered with such ease; but, as she'd suspected, being in his presence put up a barrier—on her part, at least—that made it difficult to feel anything approaching ease.

She adjusted the old-fashioned lampshade away from her face; her cheeks felt hot, as did the rest of her body. Being in the vicinity of Tim Pelham seemed to have that effect on her, darn it.

"I went to every event labeled Singles I could find," she continued. "Four or five nights a week. That was a year, let me tell you."

"This was before you met your fiancé."

Guilt attacked her again, stronger this time. Pretty soon, she would have to come clean. Friends didn't lie to each other. "Yes." Leaning in, she handed him his wine and a napkin, took her own, then sat back. She tucked her legs under her, adjusting her robe so the material covered everything.

"Well," Tim said ruefully, "these evenings have sure been an education of some sort, anyway. Thanks." He raised his glass slightly as in a toast. "To the end of number three." He sipped his wine, then nodded. "Good."

"What time did you get together with Debbie?"

"Eight."

She glanced at her watch. "But it's only nine now."

"It was brief, that's true. I told her my stomach had been upset all day and I didn't want to disgrace myself. She was very understanding." After another sip, he set his glass down. "Like I said, maybe it's me. Maybe I've been with good-time types too much, and this is what normal, regular women are like. Hey, teacher," he said with a smile, "maybe I need extra coaching."

"Please," she replied in an are-you-kidding tone. "I have a pretty good feeling you don't need to learn anything."

"I'll take that as a compliment."

"Take it however you'd like."

"Ooh," he said, clutching his stomach as though she'd put a knife in it.

They both laughed for a brief moment. Then the smile creases on Tim's face softened and disappeared entirely. He gazed at her with a sudden intensity, and all the light-heartedness in the room disappeared.

"Tell me what happened with your fiancé—with Charles. Did your eyes meet across the room? Is that how you found each other?"

*Uh-oh,* Sarah said silently, as more and more guilt piled on top of the previous load. How, she wondered, had she gotten herself in such a tangled mess, when all she really wanted to do was live a normal, honest, aboveboard, man-less existence? Sighing, she looked down at her lap, smoothed away some wrinkles in her robe, then looked back at Tim. It was best to come clean at once.

"Tim, I think we're becoming friends. Aren't we?"

After a moment's hesitation, he answered thoughtfully, "I suppose we are, yes."

"Then I need to make a confession, and hope you'll understand that I didn't— I mean, I don't—" She sighed. "Oh, never mind. Here it is: I'm not really engaged. I mean, not anymore."

## 6

He went completely still; she had the unnerving sensation that she was staring at a statue. The illusion was undone in the next moment when his eyebrows formed into a deep frown. "You're not?"

"No. I was engaged, but I walked in on Charles and another woman in bed together. There was no mistaking what they were doing. It was like a scene from a bad play—the classic betrayal." She attempted lightness in that last sentence, but she knew her tone gave her away. It had not been a pretty picture. Still, it felt good to get it out in the open at last. She hated lies.

"What happened then?" Tim asked.

"Charles looked uncomfortable for a moment, then rushed to assure me it wasn't serious—just a little roll in the hay, a physical thing, nothing to do with him and me, with that 'special bond' we had." She shook her head, reliving the moment but feeling less agitated than she usually did when thinking about that night. She looked at Tim and let out a sardonic laugh. "Can you believe it? He honestly thought I'd buy that one—that it wasn't *personal*, just a little *im*personal quickie. But, no sale. I gave him his ring and that was that."

She paused, then added quietly, "No, that wasn't that. I was pretty bitter. It hurt like crazy."

"I'll bet it did. How long ago was this?"

"Six months. Almost seven."

He stared at her for a little while, and she found herself wanting to squirm with discomfort under his unsmiling scrutiny. Finally he leaned in and rested his elbows on his knees. "Why did you say you were engaged?"

"In class? I said it to let them know that the technique works. Which it does, often."

"No. Afterward, when you and I talked. Why didn't you set me straight then?"

She couldn't tell if he was angry with her or just curious; his face revealed nothing. "I'm not sure. No, that's not it. I felt..." God, this was difficult. "It felt safer that way."

"What felt safer?"

"I wanted people, men, to leave me alone."

"All men? Or just me?"

Averting her gaze from his, Sarah observed the way her thumb moved back and forth along a seam in the chair's fabric. She wanted to hide, to run away, to escape his eyes and the way they seemed to peer into her soul.

She'd felt the same way standing in the quad with him all those years ago—disturbed, attracted, guilty, as confused as she'd ever been.

"No," she said truthfully. "It was just with you. I had this strong sense that I needed protection from you."

"Protection? Why?"

Closing her eyes, she shook her head. "Enough. No more interrogation."

"Come on, you've started, tell me all of it."

Was that annoyance she heard in his voice? Impatience? Who could blame him? She'd been evasive, both fifteen years ago and tonight.

But she was a grown woman now, and grown women dealt with things as they happened—they didn't run away. She forced herself to open her eyes and look straight at him. "Tim, the truth is, I have this bad feeling about you."

"Bad?" He seemed surprised.

She waved her hands. "No, not that *you're* bad, but bad for me. That I'd be smart to stay away from you, that's all. And so I tried to make you stay away from me."

Tim felt his jaw muscles clench. Something akin to hurt landed in his gut. He was bad for her? She'd been smart to stay away? What was he being accused of? What was his sin?

He watched while Sarah reached for her glass and downed the rest of the wine, then closed her eyes again, as though the room had begun to spin. She puzzled him. Tim continued to gaze at her; the only sound in the room was the crackling and occasional popping of the logs.

After a little while, she opened her eyes and said, "Are you angry at me?" She sounded like an apprehensive little girl, and he felt the tension in his jaw lessening. What the hell had he done to cause her to be frightened of him?

"Angry?" He considered it. She'd told the truth, so it was his turn. "Maybe. Yeah, a little. But it's more complicated than that. I think."

He paused to contemplate it some more, and an idea blew into his head like a welcome breeze on a hot, stifling day. "Hey, you know what? It just came to me. This 'bad' feeling you have—at least it's not indifference, is it? That's the good news, I guess. If you subscribe to the-glass-is-half-full philosophy."

He got up off the couch, came around the coffee table and stood before her, gazing down on her. His eyes roamed her face—the luminous gray green eyes, the smattering of freckles across her shiny nose, the general rosiness of her normally pale skin.

"No," he continued, wanting to connect with her somehow, close the gap her confession had opened between them. "It's not really anger, just more surprise. Maybe I'm a little ego-bruised that you don't trust me. But—" he grinned in spite of the seriousness of their discussion "—I'm not at all unhappy to learn that you're not taken. That means we can start all over. Fifteen years ago you were taken. Same thing the other night. Now you're not. Third date's the charm, they say."

As he bent over slightly, she sank farther into her chair. "Don't."

"Don't what?"

"I thought you were going to—" She didn't finish the sentence.

"What? Kiss you?"

She was mortified, he could tell. Without replying, she shook her head and looked down at her lap. That same feeling of hurt rose in him again. Man, she could get to him, like no other woman ever had.

"Actually," he said softly, "I was going to get myself some more wine and thought I'd pick up your glass on the way. But if you insist."

Leaning an arm on the back of her chair, he bent over and gave her a soft, noninvasive, kiss. He'd intended for it to be quick and casual, but it lasted for several heartbeats.

His lips burned from the contact. He'd heard about this kind of reaction before, but had never actually experienced it. When he forced himself to pull away, his mouth felt deprived. He wanted a lot more from Sarah Dann.

Shaken, but unwilling for her to see it, Tim walked over to the sideboard with both their glasses. Man, was he glad his back was to her as he uncorked the bottle of wine. His hands were trembling. And all from a small, closed-mouthed brushing of lips like that. Hell, he'd meant it to tease a little, to pay her back for the lie. But the damned kiss had rattled him—a lot more than it should have. Now he would have to work at taking back control, before he blew it completely.

"Seconds for you? I mean the wine," he added lightly.

"No, thanks. I'll be going to bed soon."

There was another weighty silence then, and he smiled sardonically. "You can relax, Sarah," he said, pouring wine into his glass and jamming the cork back into the bottle. "I'm not going to suggest that I join you."

He met her startled glance in the mirror. "Not that I would turn down the invitation. I've been waiting for it for fifteen years."

Her eyes widened. "You...what? What are you talking about?"

"I've never forgotten you. Never forgotten that day when we rehearsed and then you ran away."

Her hand went to her throat. He wondered if she was aware of how vulnerable she appeared at that moment.

"Come on, Tim. There's no way you thought about me steadily for all that time. I mean—" she gestured vaguely "—you must have known a lot of women in the past fifteen years. I get that sense."

"My share, I guess, mostly when I was younger. The numbers got considerably less as I grew older." He turned to face her, leaning back against the sideboard and staring right at her.

"And yes, I thought about you. No, not all day, every day. Sometimes months went by, even a year or two, but it would come back to me at the oddest times. I'd see a woman in a magazine who reminded me of you. I'd flip through *TV Guide* and see that *Cat on a Hot Tin Roof* was playing. Or, I'd even go back to San Francisco State—I talk to the kids in the broadcasting department there sometimes—and pass the building where the drama majors used to meet, and I'd think of you."

Sarah sat frozen in her seat, astonished by his revelation. Lord! All this time? Had he truly thought about her all these years? The way she had—on and off—thought about him? She clutched at the collar of her robe, her heart racing something fierce as, leaving the wineglasses on the sideboard, he walked slowly toward her.

"I've never quite gotten you out of my mind," he said.

When he reached her chair, he grasped the arms and bent over slightly, effectively imprisoning her with his body. In the firelight, his tanned skin took on a golden hue, and his startling blue eyes pierced her. His presence seemed overwhelmingly, intimidatingly masculine. She could see the passion in his eyes, feel her own body respond with a rush of heat.

"I've never really forgotten you," he whispered. "Never quite given up the yearning to—"

Her mouth parted involuntarily, and she ran her tongue over her dry lips. His answering intake of breath sent another rush of heat through her blood.

"The yearning to what?" she asked, her voice as soft, as breathless as his.

"To taste you," he whispered.

Leaning over even farther, till his mouth was inches from hers, he seemed to be waiting for her to say "Don't" or "Stop." She said nothing. She felt her lids grow heavy with sensuality, and sensed her body's acquiescence even before she offered her mouth to him.

With a guttural sound from the back of his throat, Tim took her up on her invitation. But he didn't kiss her lips—not yet.

His lips began a lazy journey across her face, tracing along her temples, over her closed lids, down her cheeks. She shivered faintly, sensed the gradual softening of her body even as she arched to meet him. Something twisted inside her when his warm breath fluttered over her mouth. With an instant jolt of reaction, her lips parted at the first touch. As he increased the pressure, degree by agonizing degree, her hands shot up to clutch his arms.

An inner warning voice was trying to say something to

her, but how could she hear anything with this steady roaring in her ears? She gripped him for balance but no matter how desperately she clung, the world kept spinning. Caution had gone up in smoke.

Was she this hungry for contact with him? Or had it simply been too long since she'd felt the comfort of an embrace, or tasted genuine desire on a man's lips? She had no answers; with a quick, helpless moan, she gave herself over to pure sensation. His mouth drank and drew from hers. His tongue and teeth drove the kiss into greater intimacies.

Without breaking their connection, Tim grabbed Sarah by the arms and pulled her up, so that her body was pressing into his. With his hands splayed across her back, he brushed his thumbs along the sides of her breasts. Still he kissed her and still the blood swam in her head.

And still that voice of warning whispered in her ear. He was playing her like an instrument, it said. It was practiced seduction, it murmured, and some men were really good at it. Sarah felt torn between the voice and the eager response of her body; she was balanced on a high, thin ledge and trying not to go over.

Now his thumbs were lightly teasing her nipples into diamond-hard points. She felt the bulge of his arousal pressing into her stomach. Gradually, through the mist of sensation, she allowed the warning thoughts to surface and hold. The liquid warmth that had been spreading through her hardened.

Breaking the kiss, she thrust Tim's hands away from her. He drew back to look at her, confusion and surprise on his face. His skin was as flushed as hers felt and he was breathing quickly.

"Whew," he exclaimed. He lifted a hand to rub his knuckles over her cheek. "That took off pretty fast, didn't it?"

"You might say that," she managed.

"However, if you're willing to give it another shot—" pulling her toward him, he angled his head "—I'm willing to take it a little slower."

Sarah averted her face. "No, don't."

It came out weakly. She had almost no reserves left and she knew it. He planted small, teasing kisses on her neck; they felt like tiny pinpricks of electricity, sending warm shock waves through her body. Fighting the strong impulse to soften once again against his hard, muscular chest, she said, "Please, Tim," pivoted away from him and walked over to the sideboard. Once there, she grabbed the edge to steady herself and met his gaze in the mirror.

He seemed puzzled by her actions. Frowning, he rubbed his fingers over his chin as though thinking. Finally, he held up his hands in mock surrender and grinned. "Okay, I got it, loud and clear. I'm not happy about it, but I got it. Is this where I leave? Or shall I pour us both another glass of wine and we can talk a little?"

"I'm kind of tired."

He nodded, then headed toward the door. She watched his progress in the mirror, until he moved out of the frame, but she was still unwilling to turn and actually face him.

"I'll call you tomorrow, okay?" he asked.

In a voice that quivered way too much, she replied, "Please, don't." She forced herself to turn around and meet him head-on.

The front door was slightly ajar and his hand was on the doorknob, as though she'd surprised him in the act of leaving. "Excuse me?"

"I said please, don't call me. Here, I mean. The office will be fine. We still have a business agreement, which I'll honor."

With a frown, Tim closed the door. "Hold it. Can we

rewind the tape here? Go back about a minute? What's going on?''

Sarah leaned against the sideboard, crossing her arms under her breasts as though the action could still the rapid heartbeat that refused to go back to normal.

Never, ever, had she been kissed like that. And never, ever, had she had that kind of physical and emotional re-action to a kiss—the immediate softening, the urge to yield, to part for him and give all of herself, every molecule of muscle and flesh, to him.

She was absolutely terrified.

"Nothing is going on," she said as crisply as she could, "except I've told you to call me at my office."

"But not at home."

"Yes."

He pondered that one for a moment. "All right. If I call you at your office tomorrow, will you have dinner with me tomorrow night?"

It was her turn to pause. She wanted to shout, *Yes I'll have dinner, and anything else you'd like to do will be fine with me!*

Instead, she said, "No."

"The next night?"

She shook her head.

"Ever?" When she said nothing, Tim stared at her, his eyes narrowing. "This is a repeat, do you realize that? This is exactly what happened fifteen years ago. And I must be some kind of idiot for standing here and taking it. Again. What is it this time? Planning on getting married tomorrow and it just slipped your mind?"

"Don't, Tim."

He moved away from the door and came toward her, all the natural humor erased from his expression. Part of her wanted to meet him and throw her arms around him; the other part wished she could disappear into the woodwork.

Keeping some distance between them, he stood, his hands fisted at his sides. "Listen to me, Sarah. I'm going to say this one time only. We—you and I—just shared a kiss. For the first time in our lives. I don't know about you, but it felt real good to me. No, I take that back. I do know about you. You liked it as much as I did."

She couldn't deny it, so she remained silent.

"So," Tim continued, "here we have a man and a woman, both unencumbered, both reasonably sane and, I assume, healthy, who share a kiss that would start a forest fire in a rainstorm. Now, with one kind of woman, the man leads the way into the bedroom—or she does—and they take care of the fire right that moment. With another kind, a woman like you, I guess you're saying, you ease up, you take it easy, you get to know each other better before dealing with the fire. I thought we already knew each other pretty well, but I'm willing." His intensity eased as his mouth quirked up at the corners. "I'm not really happy about it, considering the state of my body, but I'm willing."

Without her meaning it to, her glance strayed to the rather prominent bulge between his legs, thoroughly outlined by his faded jeans. Her face flamed. She jerked her head back up and found herself staring straight into his eyes. He was not in the least embarrassed.

"See?" he demanded. "I'm being as honest as I know how. I hear you, Sarah—hell, I respect you. We need to slow down. So, here I am, willing to postpone gratification. What's the problem?"

Something about the way he'd laid it out, clearly and logically, got her dander up. Cocking a hip, she crossed her arms over her rib cage. "This is perfect. You size me up, decide which kind of woman I am, put me in the cubbyhole of the type that takes courting, offer to do so, and wonder why I'm a little put out."

"Was I too honest? Is that it?"

"I don't know. Were you? All I know is I'm insulted. Apparently I'm one of several *types*—" she spat out the word "—say, number four of ten *types*. With one kind, you get right to it. Maybe with another, you wait three days, minimum. With *my* kind, you turn me on, accept being told no like a gentleman, offer to buy a meal, but make it very clear that sooner or later we'll wind up in the sack. Am I supposed to be flattered?"

"I *was* too honest. I should have kept my mouth shut."

"It wouldn't have helped. I know you, Tim, too well. Unfortunately, you remind me just a little bit of Charles. Lots of women, lots of fun, but it's not personal. Women are *types*. I found out after we broke up that he used to keep a list of all the lovers he'd had, with grades. I was supposed to be flattered that I was right up there with the best."

His jaw tensed and she knew he was not pleased. "And I'm paying for how that son of a bitch treated you now, aren't I? Or do you honestly think I'm that kind of scum?"

She'd overreacted, no doubt about it; but anything was better than that earlier, meltingly helpless feeling. Her first impulse was to reach out to him in apology, but that might encourage him; instead, she clasped her hands under her chin and sighed.

"No, you're not. To be fair, I think you're basically a nicer person than Charles ever was or could be. And maybe I am taking my anger at him out on you. Or maybe it's just too soon since the breakup. I don't know, but you do remind me of him in too many other ways—same age, no history of commitments to women for any length of time, a really charming man who might be just a little too charming.

"I won't be one of a list, Tim. I won't take that chance."

"What kind of chance are you talking about?"

"Of caring too much and getting my heart broken."

He put both hands, palms out, in front of his chest. "Hold it. How'd we get from being turned on to you getting your heart broken? Aren't you moving a little too swiftly?"

"It's a female thing. We project ahead when it comes to relationships. Which is why I'm protecting myself. If you're driving and you see a curve ahead, you slow down, right? If you see that the curve leads to a dead end, you go off in a different direction. It's just common sense."

"And I'm a dead end," he said. There wasn't a hint of that easygoing, laid-back nature of his in evidence. Tim Pelham was very, very angry. It was in his eyes and the set of his jaw, in the way his mouth firmed into a straight, hard line and his fists clenched and unclenched at his sides. "Excuse me if I don't feel too pleased about being called that."

He turned, pulled open the door, walked through it and slammed it behind him.

# 7

—◄◄——

"Come on," Tammi said, looking back at Tim with a quick grin. "We're down front."

Fine body, he thought with a connoisseur's appreciation, eyeing her skirt swishing back and forth as she pulled him along toward the front of the chapel. Tammi had short black hair and wore large earrings and a coral silk dress, cut very low in both front and back.

As his car was in the shop, she'd offered to pick him up. When she'd pulled up in front of his building in her shiny Camaro and he'd gotten his first look at her outfit, he'd figured there was no way she could be wearing a bra, unless it was one of those built-in jobs, and he doubted it.

"How about we sit here?" he asked her. "I like to sit in back at weddings."

"Because there's this special row for close friends. And Jeannie is my best friend in the whole world." She sounded about twelve, Tim thought, but he let her grab his hand and pull him down the aisle.

He happened to glance to his right just as Tammi was urging him toward the row on the left, and what he saw made him stop in his tracks.

Sarah.

Sitting in the same row, but across the aisle. She happened to look up at that moment, and their eyes locked. She seemed surprised to see him, then slightly flustered.

But then the same could be said for him. What was she doing here? he wondered. And why did he have to catch his breath and fight down both anger and exhilaration at the sight of her?

It had been two weeks since that night at her place, when he'd stormed out of there royally pissed off, stung by her condemnation of him. He'd gone straight to Sully's, gotten pie-eyed, and had woken up the next day still riled and with a beaut of a headache on top of it.

He'd spent a week keeping the anger alive, then—determined to shut Sarah Dann out of his mind—had called number four on the list, Tammi Greene. They'd met and had an okay time. She was pretty much a lightweight, brain-wise, but easy to look at and fun. So he'd asked her out again, and she'd suggested he be her date for her friend's wedding, so he was here today.

As was Sarah. Had he known...

Turning away deliberately, he followed Tammi to their seats.

"You think it's just the most romantic thing you've ever heard of?"

"Pardon?" he said a few minutes later.

"You haven't been listening, naughty boy," Tammi chuckled with a light punch to his arm. "I was telling you about how they met."

"How who met?"

"Jeannie and Roger. The bride and groom," she added, less playfully now, and he couldn't blame her. He'd forgotten her existence since seeing Sarah.

"Oh, yeah, sorry. Okay, how did they meet?"

"In that class. You know, the one we both took? Meet Your Mate? Jeannie met Roger there four months ago— they were practice partners. Isn't that like fate? And he asked her out right away, and here it is, their wedding day." She sighed dramatically. "And it's just like in the fairy tales. That's why I signed up for the class, because of the luck Jeannie had.''

"I see. Did you notice the teacher is here?"

"Really? Where?" She craned her neck, looking around.

Tim pointed across the aisle. "There, the redhead in the green suit."

Tammi frowned. "She wasn't my teacher. Dotti was blond and real skinny, like she works out all the time. Who's she?"

"Sarah Dann. Oh, yeah, that's right. She was the substitute the night I took the class."

Dismissing the woman across the aisle with a disinterested shrug, Tammi smiled up at him, a dimple forming in one cheek. "Are you like the rest of us? Did you take the class to meet someone?"

"Not at the time." He tugged at his tie; he'd made it too tight. "It was a gift from a friend, actually."

"Well, I'm sure glad it was." She moved a little closer to him and slid her hand through his bent elbow. "Because the two of us are here right now, aren't we?" Somehow her position set his arm against the side of her breast. Soft yet firm at the same time. And she was definitely not wearing a bra.

Tammi's invitation was subtle but unmistakable, and usually he didn't mind aggressive women; liked them, actually. Tammi was fine looking and was obviously interested in him physically. But at the moment, he couldn't return the interest.

Not having kissed Sarah.

He snuck a peek over to her side of the aisle. She was staring straight ahead and wore a dark green jacket over a matching long skirt. A hint of a pale beige scoop-necked blouse with lace at the neckline showed in the V of her jacket. Her hair was pulled back into a knot at her neck and small gold hoops glistened at her ears.

Tammi looked like a lush, open invitation; Sarah looked closed and self-sufficient. But he found her three times as sexy as the woman sitting by his side. Why? he wondered, not for the first time. What was it about her?

His musings were interrupted by organ music and the sound of children giggling. The ceremony had begun.

Sarah wanted out of there, a whole lot. Why she had agreed to attend the wedding, she didn't know. She hadn't even taught the class in which the bride and groom had met. But she was covering for Dotti, the still-recuperating teacher; besides, it was policy that someone from Keep On Learning attended all weddings resulting from her class. It was good PR. So, she was here.

As was Tim, and she wished he weren't. He distracted her, made her nervous. And she couldn't seem to stop herself from glancing over at him when she was pretty sure he wasn't watching. He looked absolutely wonderful in a navy suit, crisp white shirt and multicolored tie. She hadn't seen him all spiffed up before. His usual dress was California casual—jeans, sweaters, T-shirts—but today he looked like a *Gentlemen's Quarterly* model, with his tan, clean-shaven face and the sprinkling of silver throughout his sandy hair. She'd always been a sucker for a man in a well-cut suit—the result of some early fixation on old Cary Grant movies, she supposed.

She recognized the coquettish brunette he was with as one from the list she'd sent Tim. His date kept draping herself all over him, batting her lashes at him and squirming suggestively in her seat. Sarah found herself fantasizing, with several variations, the woman's slow, painful death.

There it was again, that jealousy. Where in the world was all this *passion* coming from? She'd been working so hard at being cool and composed. When she'd been a child, those mood swings of hers had driven her parents crazy, then had had the same effect on her husband and, later, on Charles.

She tried to focus on the ceremony—but she kept remembering her own wedding—her quaking knees, how she'd been sick to her stomach right up to the moment, the sheer terror. Her father had practically had to push her down the aisle. She'd been so young.

She also kept remembering that night two weeks ago; she could still taste Tim and his mouth, still recollect the way her very skin had come alive at his touch. Shivering involuntarily, she wished they would get to the "I dos" as quickly as possible.

After the happy couple had declared their undying love and proceeded to the back of the chapel, Sarah considered making an early evening of it. However, if she was truly going to do some publicity for Keep On Learning, she would have to show up at the reception. So, ignoring Tim the way he seemed to be ignoring her, she steeled herself to do just that.

The wedding celebration was held in Marin County, at a two-story, glassed-in restaurant with a wide deck that jutted out into the bay. Sarah was not at Tim's table, thank heavens, so she managed to avoid him for quite a while, calling herself all kinds of names the whole time. Why couldn't she face him, make some conversation, be friendly? Hadn't they become friends—at least before they'd kissed?

But that had changed everything.

She was on the deck, standing by the railing and gazing at the beginnings of a golden sunset, when she caught a movement out of the corner of her eye. Tim had just walked up to the railing and was now standing about twenty feet away, also peering out at the water. He was alone, his jacket slung behind him, hooked by an index finger; his other elbow rested on the rail. Loud, festive music and laughter was blaring from the restaurant behind them, but only the two of them were here at this moment.

"I got the message about the show," she said, deciding to make an attempt at conversation but having to raise her voice to be heard over the competing noise from the party.

He turned toward her. "Excuse me?"

"Tomorrow. I got your message that I'm booked on 'The Don Morrisey Show' tomorrow, to be interviewed about the school. Thanks."

"You're welcome. It's all part of the deal." He smiled impersonally, then turned his head and gazed out again.

Okay, he was ignoring her overture. She could live with that.

Apparently she couldn't, though, and found herself moving a few steps closer to him. "Your date," she said. "She was on the list, wasn't she?"

"Sure was. We've been out twice, actually."

"Oh, good. At least one name worked out okay. I'm relieved."

*Have you slept with her? Did you like it?*

Both of these questions resounded in her head, but she figured they were in pretty bad taste, so she kept them there.

"She seems nice," she offered instead.

"She is."

"A lively personality."

"Yes."

A silence followed. He didn't want to talk, it was obvious. So, why didn't she leave it at that? Ego? A challenge? Sarah had no idea, but she had an urge to get some sort of reaction from Tim other than those shielded, polite responses. "She's pretty, too."

"Sure is."

"And that's a great dress she's wearing."

"Or almost wearing," he said.

He turned his head; their glances met and they both laughed.

Tim took a few steps closer to her, then folded his jacket across the railing. "You, on the other hand," he continued, "are buttoned up in a suit once again."

Stung by his words, she turned and gazed out at a sailboat drifting lazily in the distance. He'd meant that as some kind of zinger, she was pretty sure; some kind of observation about women who dressed to please men—as Tammi did and she did not.

"Hey, no." Tim moved a little closer still. "It's a great suit, you look terrific in suits. I didn't mean it as a criticism."

Shrugging, she said, "Sure, you did, but it's true. Most of my wardrobe consists of business clothing. I haven't bought a real, honest-to-God party dress in ages. Not since, well, you know…Charles."

"Then you're due, aren't you?"

"I guess I am."

In the silence that followed this exchange, Sarah noted how soft and soothing the waves were, how the Pacific Ocean seemed to have its own distinct shades of gray and blue and green and occasionally all three, how the air was especially clear today.

And how the man at her side seemed to give off a special kind of energy that reached out to her and enveloped her completely.

Leaning both elbows on the rail, Tim focused his attention on something out at sea. "Tell me, do you think the happy couple will make it?"

"I think they have a chance."

"Another female thing? Second sight?"

"I've made a study of compatibility. My major was psychology."

"So you went to college, after all? Back to San Francisco State? I never saw you around."

"No. I wound up at a smaller school."

*Because of you,* she almost said. *Because of how incredibly turned on you made me feel, just before I got married. God help me, I even thought of you on my wedding night, and I was a virgin.*

But she didn't say that. Would not give him any more insider information to use in his campaign to bed her.

If there even was a campaign by now, she added wryly. Tim seemed to be doing just fine with ol' silicone Tammi. No one, Sarah mused, feeling only mildly ashamed of her mean-spiritedness but unable to help it, no one stood that high and pointy without additives.

"Well," she said, "I guess I'd better be getting back to the party."

"I think I'll stay out here a little longer."

"Aren't you having a good time?"

"I'm not too nuts about weddings." He grinned ruefully. "They seem to make my collar feel too tight and my hands clammy."

"What a surprise."

Tim felt a wave of irritation at her sarcasm, even though he'd fed her the straight line. "You really think you have me figured out, don't you? And you talk about me categorizing women."

She held her hands up, palms out. "I deserved that. I'm sorry, Tim. Really I am."

He wasn't expecting her apology, and it threw him. "No, it was my fault."

"No, it was mine."

"Stop! You're both right!" he pronounced in a perfect imitation of a slick game-show host.

She laughed, and he smiled back.

He sure liked her face when it was happy. He sure liked

her, period. Whatever craziness went on between them, he genuinely enjoyed this woman's company.

"Sarah, I—" he began.

"There you are," Tammi said, heading his way along the deck from behind Sarah, but ignoring her. Coral skirts swished and rustled as she moved, then she planted herself right in front of him. "I've been wondering where you were. You promised to dance with me."

After a quick, apologetic glance at Sarah, he said to Tammi, "So I did," and allowed her to lead him back into the restaurant.

For the next half hour or so, he tried to be a decent, attentive date, but the louder and more raucous the celebration became, the more he didn't feel like participating. He also kept looking around for Sarah, and when he lost sight of her for any length of time, got downright dejected. Damn. He was still drawn to the woman like a magnet. Something would have to be done about this.

At one point, while he was craning his neck to try to find Sarah in the crowd, Tammi tapped him on the shoulder. "Tim? Did you hear me?"

"Huh?"

"I want to dance again," she told him, her mouth drawn down in a pout. "This is supposed to be a party. We're supposed to be having fun."

"I'm sorry," he said. And he was.

"Why, I'll be honored to dance with you, Ms. Tammi," said the groom's best man in a fake Southern-gentleman accent, as he passed their table. He'd been eyeing her all afternoon, Tim had observed without much caring, and he was welcome to her. "Y'all come on."

With a giggle, Tammi gathered her skirts and allowed herself to be swept onto the dance floor.

The sky was streaked now with ribbons of gold and pink as the sun made its way to another part of the world. Sarah was outside again, seated by herself at a round table. For some indefinable reason, she felt about as lonely as she'd ever felt in her life.

Maybe it was because everybody inside seemed to be part of a couple. Even Tim was with someone, on their second date, dancing his feet off. Sarah's reaction, when that Tammi person had dragged him away, had been a mixture of helplessness and an urge to get a club and fight her for possession. It had shaken her to the core; had made her realize Tim was—in spite of all her efforts—*very* important to her.

Her body had been aching for him since she'd set eyes on him earlier, back at the church. No, the truth now. She'd been aching for him since he'd kissed her. She had never felt that kind of strong sensual urge toward a man before— not even toward Charles. And it was overwhelming.

She craved him; or rather, her body did, for sure, and part of her mind. Craved him like a chocoholic craved a pound of Mrs. See's finest.

A while ago, when she and Tim had stood here, on the deck, and skirted around all the unspoken issues between them, in one part of her brain she'd fantasized him doing a slow striptease for her.

He would remove his shirt, button by button, his eyes locking on hers and never moving. And then he would run his hand over his chest and abdomen, until his fingers touched the top of his zipper. At that point, he would slow down even more.

He would, in fact, probably taunt her and tease her till she practically sobbed for him to take her. And she would let him take her; demand it, actually....

The moment he arrived on the deck, Tim understood the seemingly obscure urge that had drawn him there. Sarah sat at a table near the railing. She had taken off her jacket, which was draped over the chair back. What he'd thought was a lace-trimmed blouse turned out to be a revealing cream-colored camisole with thin straps.

As she gazed out, her elbow rested on the tabletop and she played absently with one of the straps. Without the jacket, he could see how nicely rounded her arms were, and how even more nicely rounded her breasts were, with their creamy-white tops and—he drew in a breath—the stiff, jutting points thrusting against the silk.

Oh, man, he wanted her. It might have been the cooling night air that made her nipples hard; but with that dreamy look on her face, and the way the tips of her fingernails grazed lightly over the skin around the silk fabric, he didn't think so.

His hands itched to cup those lovely, full mounds and make her cry out with pleasure. As he felt himself growing hard, he cursed silently. He'd heard about men feeling powerless over their attraction to a woman, but he'd never experienced it before. It scared him, took control away from him. Which he did not like in the least.

But there it was—a fact. And there she was, in fact. And if he was about to set some sort of record for pursuing an unwilling female, then so be it.

As he came up behind her, an almost-overwhelming muskiness filled his nostrils, and he knew it was part floral wedding decoration, part Sarah, and part the result of his body's instinctive, primitive urge toward this woman.

As she felt a man's hands on her shoulders, Sarah gasped. But not with fright. She knew who those hands belonged to. Her fantasies had willed him to come to her.

Her body went all tingly at his touch. Her breathing and heartbeat seemed to stop, and then it all started up again twice as fast. She remained gazing out to sea for a moment longer, then angled her head around and studied his face.

What she saw in his startlingly blue eyes—the intensity of the raw, naked hunger there—made something slide into place in her head.

She'd wished for him and he was there. There was no need to fight anymore, because what happened was now out of her hands, and in the lap of the gods. Click. It was decided.

Facing the ocean again, Sarah sat back in her chair, her body relaxing under his palms. He was offering and she was acquiescing; they were both passing silent messages back and forth that what was happening was more than just the placement of a man's hands on a woman's bare skin. She reveled in the silent messages, reveled in feeling like a thoroughly desirable, full-blooded woman.

"It's an incredible sunset," she said quietly.

He bent over and whispered in her ear, "I know where there's an even better view."

She smiled to herself. "Impossible."

He rubbed his mouth over the skin on the back of her neck, and the tingling grew more pronounced. His lips felt warm and promising.

"Trust me," he said. "Come with me." It was a statement, not a question. Still...

"What about your date?" she asked in a low voice.

"She's been taken over by the best man. He's much better for her, really. He's been after her all day. I, on the other hand, am completely indifferent to her."

"Are you?"

"Most definitely." He straightened and came around, perching a hip on the table and obscuring her view. With a finger, he brought her chin up so they could look right into each other's eyes. "I seem to have someone else in my head and she won't go away, no matter what I do. I'm not sorry."

She stared at him for a long, pulsating moment, then nodded slowly. "Me neither."

Reaching up, she stroked her fingers down the side of his cheek. He quivered, then grabbed her hand, holding the palm flat against his face. She loved touching him.

"Where is this fabulous view?" she asked with a smile.

"My place."

The two words hung out there in the air, and Sarah and Tim gazed at each other with the final unspoken question and answer in their eyes.

There wasn't even a struggle on her part. She removed her hand from under his and reached behind her for her jacket.

"We'd better hurry then, hadn't we?" she said. "The sun will be down in a half hour."

The ride to Tim's place had an odd sense of unreality about it. The moment he'd taken her hand at the restaurant, Sarah had gone into a state of dreaminess that rendered her incapable of much concentration.

Tim seemed to be in a similar mood, as neither of them said a word during the entire ride. They touched, though. He drove her Miata and, in between shifting from one gear to another, he held her hand on the armrest that separated their seats, sometimes stroking her wrist or playing with her fingers.

She luxuriated in the contact. She was hungry—for a man's touch, for physical sensation, for closeness and cuddling and the sense of being alive that sex brought. She was hungry for Tim, but she was going to his condo with him with eyes wide open.

There would be no future to what happened today, and she was to expect none. No one had coaxed or dared or maneuvered her into this; there would be none of that "I couldn't help myself" nonsense afterward. Ignoring a small dart of sadness these thoughts brought, Sarah smiled. It was such a relief not to feel ambivalent for once.

Life was good. The weather was gorgeous. The top was down and she removed the pins from her bun so her hair could blow wild and free. The Golden Gate Bridge at sunset was truly breathtaking, all pale rusts and golds. The magical

city of San Francisco stretched out before them—its narrow
streets lined with colorful old houses and shops, the hills
that rose and fell like a huge, never-ending roller coaster.

Eventually they pulled up in front of a new-looking,
white concrete building ringed on all floors by plant-filled
balconies. Tim helped her out of the car, returned her keys,
and—smiling but still not saying a word—led her to the
elevator at one end of the marble lobby. Inside were three
other people. Tim draped his arm around her and drew her
close. With her head resting on his shoulder, she could
smell the light wool of his jacket and the fresh air from the
car ride.

When he gazed down on her for a moment, her breathing
quickened; the intensity in his sky blue eyes was back. A
muscle in his jaw tensed, she felt his arm tighten around
her, and her heart rate sped up even more. It was as though
she could read his mind, knew how much he desired her,
and her body's deep interior muscles responded by clench-
ing in readiness.

Once they were in his apartment, she barely had time to
register a large, white-walled living room—and, as Tim had
promised, an astonishing view of the city's skyline at the
end of sunset—before he closed the door behind them and
backed her against the wall.

He brushed his fingers over her cheeks, then combed
them through her hair, now freed from the tidy bun she'd
worked on so hard just that morning.

"I want you," he said, his body pressing into hers. His
heart drummed fast and hard against hers, but the quiet
solemnity of his statement made her smile even as his lips
cruised over her face.

"And I want you."

"Do you?"

In his eyes she thought she saw, along with the hunger,
something else. Could it be a small kernel of doubt, even

fear of what her answer would be? Impossible, she thought. Not Tim.

In the next instant it was gone, and she decided it had been her imagination. But the thought—the possibility—of Tim Pelham being vulnerable to her not only surprised her; it touched her, in a place she did not want to be touched.

Averting her gaze, she murmured "Very much," as her body trembled and arched under his. She brought her hands up under his jacket, her fingers skimming over the soft, fine linen of his shirt, exploring the intriguing ripple of muscle beneath.

He gripped the sides of her head so she was forced to look right at him. "It's not simple with you, you know," he said. "Nothing is simple with you."

"You talk too much."

Still solemn, he studied her for a brief moment. Then he smiled, and tiny licks of fire leaped just below her stomach. She took his hands, placed them around her waist, and offered her mouth to him. When he kissed her, she showed him with her lips and tongue what she didn't want to say with words.

Tim felt himself literally shaking with need for her—fifteen years of it—which was lucky, because her need was obviously just as strong. Still, he wanted to put the brakes on, to savor these first moments of discovery.

However, Sarah's generous mouth, her moist tongue, pulled him under, sucked him in. She seemed greedy and not at all willing to slow the pace down. It was as though she was searching for what he had always looked for in other women—simple, hot, mutual pleasure.

He wanted to stop, to tell her how pleasing he found her, how special this moment was, that she was not just any woman. But she'd as good as told him not to talk. He figured he knew when to shut up as well as the next man.

Responding to her urgency, Tim tugged off her jacket

while she went to work on his shirt buttons. The action
moved them away from the wall, and he stumbled against
the back of an easy chair. He laughed, and so did she, but
only for a moment. She began removing her own clothes
immediately, so he did the same with his.

The bedroom was too damn far, so, perching on the arm
of his large couch, he pulled her to him so she stood between his legs. Then he feasted on her. She was rounded
yet firm, her skin a pale gold color with scattered freckles
in intriguing places, and soft as a rose petal. He fell backward onto the couch and drew her on top of him.

She tasted of honey and sweet oil, but he barely had time
to register all the other sensations of her body as she
streaked mindlessly into heat, devouring his desire the way
a dehydrated woman might lap up raindrops. She demanded
pleasure from him and he gave it, his mouth moving all
over her hollows and rounded curves, finding the places
that made her squirm and then making her squirm even
more.

No thoughts, Sarah swore. No emotions. She was pursuing physical pleasure from a man, nothing more. She
needed this, all these sensations, she told herself as she
spiraled higher and higher in response to his hands, his
mouth, his tongue. She felt wild and reckless, and when he
drove her to an intense, knife-edged orgasm, she cried out,
her body trembling with the aftereffects of a powerful, unexpected eruption.

She could hear his hard, strained breathing even as his
hands and mouth began to slow down. He murmured something to her, rose from the couch and was gone. She hadn't
understood the words and felt bereft at the loss of his warm,
powerful, giving body. She fought down the urge to call to
him. He returned almost immediately, holding a foil-
wrapped condom in his hand.

"Tim, thank you." She held out her arms to him; she

wanted to hug him tightly and weep with gratitude that he'd thought of protection when she had not. Surrender. Surprise. Loss. Relief. Tears. She'd run the emotional gamut in a matter of minutes. More emotions were trying to sneak through even now.

*No,* she told herself. *No.* Quickly, even fiercely, she moved to block them off. Even as his lips whispered over hers, she was cupping his buttocks and pulling him toward her spread legs. His body went rigid as she took him into her hot grasp.

He just had time to put on the condom when she locked her legs around his hips. She thought she heard him say, ''Wait,'' but she was already surrounding him, already drawing him deep into that part of her that still ached to be filled, already urging him to match her frantic rhythm. Together they raced toward release, their bodies' demands too overwhelming for anything else.

Afterward, he lay sprawled over her on the couch, both of them panting. Tim knew he was heavy on her, but he wasn't ready to move, or to look at her, to meet her eyes. Good sex, he thought. Fantastic sex.

Empty sex.

Minus all those things called emotions. Which he never felt, not ever.

Still, he had the sensation of having been— What was the word? *Used.* He, Tim Pelham, who had always taken whatever a woman offered with an easy shrug and no backward looks, had felt used.

Payback, he thought. The first time he had wanted more from a woman, he had run up against one who wasn't interested. Not at present, at least.

However, he reminded himself with a smile, the night was young. The next time would be in the bedroom, on his large, comfortable bed. It would be leisurely. He would take the lead, no matter what. Whatever happened would be infinitely more satisfying than their first encounter had been. He was looking forward to it.

Tim eased himself off Sarah, then lay on his side, his elbow bent, his head resting on his hand. Lightly, his fingertips traced the ridge of her collarbone.

Slow. Deliberate. That's how it would be. He felt his body hardening already at the mere thought of what was ahead.

"Sarah—" he began.

She scrambled up from the couch as though he'd turned on a sudden light switch. "Do you have any tea? I think I'd like some tea." Grabbing an afghan that was draped over a hassock, she wrapped it around herself. "Where is the powder room?"

"Down the hall, first door to the right. Are you okay?" When she nodded quickly, he said, "There's a robe hanging in there, if you want. Do you really want tea? Now?"

When she nodded again, adamantly, he said, "Then I'll heat up the water."

He put his briefs on, then headed for his small-but-thoroughly-modern kitchen. She needed him to be gentle, he told himself, not pushy. Sarah had a little trust problem, she'd made that clear; she found him a little too... "charming" was the word she'd used.

Did she mean slick, too practiced? Even jaded? He frowned. He wasn't that way, he didn't think; but still, he didn't want to scare her off.

When Sarah entered the kitchen, wearing Tim's terry cloth robe and feeling edgy and distracted, he looked up from the counter where three different boxes of tea bags lay. He grinned. "I actually have some, but I'm not sure how old. Tea doesn't go bad, does it?"

He held out one of the boxes and she took it, although she wasn't quite sure why. It wasn't as if she could tell if it had turned, or whatever tea did when it got old. The kettle whistled and Tim shut it off, then came up behind her and, putting his arms around her waist, kissed her neck.

She stiffened automatically and his movements stilled. Then he withdrew his arms and busied himself filling cups with hot water and tea bags. "So, you're a tea drinker."

She didn't know what she was, at the moment. In a foggy state, removed, confused. She hugged herself. She felt sore and swollen and trembly.

Also hollow inside.

"I find it soothes me," she said.

He glanced over his shoulder, and one corner of his mouth quirked up. "You need soothing, I'd like to apply for the job."

Instead of answering, she sat down at the built-in breakfast nook, wrapping his robe even tighter around her. She felt cold, so cold.

She fought the urge to talk to Tim; to talk about what had just happened and all her fears. The more she was with him, the more she could feel a corner of her armor peeling away like the frayed edge of old wallpaper. And she really didn't want that. She couldn't let it happen. In the past hour, she'd had a glimpse of something deeper, something important, before she'd shut it out.

He set both cups on the table, but remained standing. "What is it, Sarah?"

She shrugged and took a sip of her tea. It was hot, and not very strong. Cupping both hands around the heated porcelain, she focused her attention on the pale brown liquid. "I did it again."

"Did what again?"

"Made the wrong decision. I thought this—being with you, all of it—would be okay," she said thoughtfully. "But I guess I was fooling myself."

"About what?"

"I'm...not comfortable with casual sex."

For a moment, he didn't reply. Then he leaned a hand on the table and said, "Casual sex? You call what just happened casual?"

"Call it what you like." The defeated monotone of her own voice reflected the way she felt inside. "Casual sex, recreational, no strings, no ties, 'It was just one of those things.'" She looked up at him. "Wasn't it?"

He studied her for another moment. "Maybe. In a way. But you're the one saying it. Not me."

"But you will. Eventually."

"How do you know?"

"I just know, that's all." It was a weak, stupid response, but it was all she had.

She sensed his annoyance even though he didn't express it. Instead, he pulled the other chair out from the table, sat down, seemed to deliberate something in his head, then expelled a breath.

His gaze probed hers intensely, but his tone was quiet and controlled when he asked, "What is it you want, Sarah? A contract? A formal list of my intentions? Only serious, marriage-minded men need apply for the pleasure of your body?" He held his hands out, raised and lowered his shoulders. "It's all a possibility, sure, but if you want guarantees, you've come to the wrong guy."

"Exactly."

"What I mean is we take it one step at a time and see what happens."

"No, we don't."

When that telltale muscle in his jaw clenched, she covered his hand with hers. "Tim, it's not you. Really it's not. It's me. My track record stinks. I don't trust myself, my gut, my decision making. I've made too many bad ones.

"I was pushed around by my parents and never stood up to them, never had an opinion of my own. I went into a disastrous marriage, drove myself nuts before I got out of it, and later, when I thought I was finally coming into my own, picked an even more disastrous man to get engaged to. I've learned my lesson. When it comes to men, my radar is faulty. My heart—I can't trust it. It's let me down too many times. Which is why I need to take a lot of care.''

"I understand, but—"

"I want it all," she continued, interrupting him. It was important, crucial, that he understand. There were tears threatening, but she held them back. "I want a career, Tim. And I want a husband, a home, kids. The whole package. I've wanted it my whole life. But I don't handle disappointment and hurt too well. If I get involved with one more disaster, I just know I'll close up forever. There's a real potential for disaster when you indulge in sex that means nothing.''

"This meant nothing?"

Oh, no. Had she hurt him? Again? Hit him in the ego? She hadn't intended to.

"No, it was terrific. I mean, you're a great lover, really." She splayed her hand across her chest. "I thought my heart would... Well, I don't think I've ever reacted that quickly to anything. It felt like—" She stopped. "But, I can't—" She tried again, but couldn't finish the sentence.

She looked down at her tea, as though it could offer answers. This was impossible, absolutely impossible. "Oh, never mind," she said, thoroughly disgusted with herself.

"Can't what?" he asked.

The tears were closer now. "Can't do this anymore!"

Agitated, frustrated, Sarah couldn't remain seated, so she jumped up, swept into the living room, gathered her clothes and hurriedly put them on. Tim stormed out of the kitchen right on her heels.

"I should never have done this," she muttered. "It was

a mistake and it's all my fault. One of these days I'm going to learn. I listened to my hormones instead of my head.''

"It was more than just hormones and you know it."

"Which makes it just that much more tantalizing and that much more possible for heartbreak." She zipped up her skirt and looked around for her shoes.

"Oh, yeah, that's right. I'm a dead end, aren't I?"

She lifted her gaze from the floor and met his. "I'm sorry," she replied, trying to placate him. "I should never have said that. I wish I could take it back. You're still angry."

"You're damned right I'm angry!" He stood right in front of her now, his hands in fists by his sides. "We do this push-pull thing and it's nuts. Saying no, no, no, then yes, yes, yes, and we get together and it's magic, and then 'Oops, I shouldn't have!' I mean, is this some new version of teasing? Is this how you get your jollies? Not real adult behavior on your part, is it?"

"Adult behavior?" The urge to cry was gone; in its place was fury at what he'd implied about her. "I'm the one who wants a permanent commitment, not you. I mean, talk about adult behavior. What kind of man has reached your age and has never had anything approaching a serious relationship? Has never, to quote you, even thought about it. If we're measuring maturity here, you're pretty low on the scale."

"A real dead end, I guess." Both his face and his tone were bitter.

"You're the one who said it this time, not me." Grabbing her jacket and purse, she headed for the door. "I sure am glad I have my own car."

"So am I."

"Why don't you call the wedding and see if Tammi's left yet. I think she's more your style."

She rushed out, slamming the door behind her. After punching the elevator button several times, she paced up and down the carpeted area, muttering to herself about the slowness of elevators, especially when you were in a hurry, and the impossibility of talking about feelings to a man. They always took everything personally.

The elevator arrived, and the doors slid open, inviting her in. But instead of entering, she stood facing it. Her body trembled with a sudden chill and she rubbed up and down her arms. What had happened in there just now? she asked herself. What had she said? How had it gotten out of hand?

Suddenly she felt foolish; she and Tim had both said some hurtful things. It couldn't be left like this. Maybe she needed to apologize. Did she? She drummed her fingers on the marble wall. The elevator doors closed, but she barely noticed.

She'd overreacted again, hadn't she? Been way too emotional. Taken Tim's head off—for nothing. What had the poor man done? She'd wanted to have sex with him, had let him know, and he'd willingly complied. Then she'd come on like some ruined virgin, all filled with regrets and self-laceration.

And she'd been so sure it wouldn't turn out like this!

Yes. She needed to apologize. It was that simple. It was the right, the responsible thing to do. What she would say, she didn't know, but she would find the words. And it had to be now, before she talked herself out of it.

Sarah retraced her steps and knocked on Tim's door. As though he'd been waiting for her, he yanked it open. In his hand he held out a lace garter belt and pale sheer stockings. She saw that he was absolutely enraged, and just keeping a lid on it.

He thrust her delicate underthings at her. "That's right. You forgot these. You may need them again sometime. Now take them and get out of here."

When she didn't move, he pointedly dropped them at her

feet and closed his door with finality. She heard the lock being yanked loudly into place.

Openmouthed, Sarah stared at the number 602 under his brass knocker for a while. Then she bent down to retrieve her things. At that moment, an elderly woman and a small poodle pranced by. The dog whined and pulled at its leash, trying to sniff Sarah's undergarments. But its owner yanked at its jeweled collar and said, "Come, Muffin. We don't want to get near the nasty things."

Sarah winced, stared down at her lovely new garter belt and extremely expensive stockings, and decided to leave them just where they were. She never wanted to be reminded of Tim Pelham again.

# 9

Sarah had forgotten about the next day, however—about her radio interview on "The Don Morrisey Show." After a sleepless night, some thought was given to canceling her appearance, but on reconsideration, she decided that would make her a spineless wimp.

She would certainly try to avoid running into Tim, but just for insurance, she called Lois at 6:00 a.m. and asked her to accompany her to the radio station. Lois, who'd just returned from a pan-Pacific flight, wanted to go back to sleep, but Sarah begged her and, grumbling, Lois agreed.

At 9:45 a.m., the two friends approached the glass doors of KCAW Radio, located on the top floor of one of San Francisco's tallest buildings.

"Hey, Sarah, you sure you want me here?" Lois asked. "I thought you were used to speaking in public and all that."

Lois wore a bright yellow sweater and miniskirt, which showed her lush figure to advantage, and her straight, honey-blond hair fell just to the tops of her shoulders. She not only didn't seem jet-lagged, she was as vibrant as always.

Sarah felt washed-out and utterly exhausted. "Yes, I'm sure. Would I ask if I wasn't sure?"

"Hey, no need to take my head off. Just asking."

"Sorry."

"You know what? You're acting like a green kid on the way to her first blind date."

"Well, I'm scared, Lo." She wiped her damp hands on her skirt, then muttered to herself. Did sweat come off silk? She'd worn a dress today—no "buttoned-up" suits, thank you, but a deep blue, classic-cut silk sheath with a slim silver belt. She pictured dark handprints all over the thing and groaned.

"It's just that I've never been on the radio before," Sarah said, "and I need all the support I can get. Please, Lo. I need you."

Lois gave her a smile and a quick hug. "Hey, honey, you need me? You got me."

Sarah looked at her friend with gratitude, then pushed open the doors to the KCAW reception area. It was a modest space, with a couple of small couches and a coffee table. The walls were decorated with plaques and awards; over the loudspeakers, a man and woman spoke of a recent trip to Prague and a restaurant they'd dined at.

Sarah went up to the receptionist and offered her name. She'd told a white lie to Lois. She knew that only some of the nervousness she was experiencing was because she was about to be interviewed on live radio. Most of it was due to fear—fear of running into Tim and what she would say if she did. Lois knew nothing about what had happened between them the previous night, and, for right now, Sarah wanted to keep it that way.

As a matter of fact, Sarah herself wasn't quite sure what had happened between her and Tim. She only knew that she'd surrendered to a strong impulse and had experienced sexual release beyond anything in her experience; that even with her body's reaction, there had been something missing; and that she'd proceeded to whine afterward about "commitment" and "relationships"—all those horrible words she was sick of from bestsellers and TV talk shows.

She'd behaved badly, she knew it, although she'd been treated pretty shabbily, too, at the end. Still, the fault was hers...

On top of which, she no longer possessed a perfectly lovely Victoria's Secret garter belt that had been a special purchase on one of her "I need a pick-me-up" days after the Charles debacle.

Okay, so she probably owed Tim an apology. Not probably, she *did* owe him an apology. But for now, she would just as soon avoid dealing with the whole thing. Now, she had to don her Successful Woman of Business persona and be amusing and interesting on the radio, so her school would sound like a fun place to be.

Sarah had never listened to "The Don Morrisey Show" before, but both Lois and Marianne said it was popular and not too terrible—more Larry King than Howard Stern. She assured herself she could handle it, nerves and all.

Studio L, the receptionist had said, so Sarah and Lois walked along a carpeted corridor lined with glassed-in studios and control booths. When they got to "L," Sarah wiped her hands on her skirt again as she peered inside.

What she saw in there was not what she'd expected, even if it was what she had feared.

Sitting at a long table on which two microphones were placed side by side, was Tim. His back was to the mikes and he was talking to a skinny young kid wearing a T-shirt that said Grunge Lives!

"Is that what Don Morrisey looks like?" Lois whispered. "The one in the chair?"

"No. That's the station manager." Sarah's heart raced in sudden panic. Why was he here? And was there a back door? "Tim Pelham."

"Tim Pelham? That's the guy you told me about, right? The one you knew a long time ago?"

"The one and only."

"Hmm."

"What do you mean, hmm?"

"Nice, that's all. Just like you described him, only cuter." Lois angled her head toward Sarah and cocked an eyebrow. "You two gotten together yet? If so, I want details."

"Don't, Lois."

"Don't what?"

"I'm nervous enough about going on the air."

"You sure that's all you're nervous about?" she drawled. "Aha. A light dawns. I wondered why you woke me out of a sorely-needed sleep and informed me that our friendship was on the line if I didn't get my butt down here to be with you. Could the reason be that very nice-looking man sitting in that room?"

Sarah narrowed her eyes at her friend. "You know me too well. Shut up."

At that moment, Tim glanced up, saw them and waved them in. Sarah had no choice but to enter, with Lois close behind.

"Transfer all that stuff to DAT," he was saying as they came into the room, "and send it off by FedEx, okay Andy?"

"It's done, Tim."

"That's today," he said with a smile. "Not tomorrow and not tonight. Today. The final mix for the 'Eclectic Acoustic' piece can wait."

"Got it. Do it now," Andy said, as though repeating the words in his head, "not tonight and not tomorrow. No problem." He scooted out of the booth, bobbing his head shyly at the two women as he did.

"Andy's a good kid," Tim said. "Lots of potential, but he gets a little lost in the music and forgets his job." He swiveled his chair so he was facing the two of them, then he stood. "Good morning, Sarah," he said pleasantly.

"Hello." She felt her stomach clench but managed to reply calmly, "Tim, this is my friend, Lois Bonner. Lois, this is Tim Pelham."

After giving Lois a quick, expert assessment, he smiled that charming smile of his and shook her hand. "Lois? It's a pleasure to meet you."

"The pleasure is *real* mutual." Lois's Southern accent seemed even more pronounced than usual.

Sarah had a sudden vision of both Tim and Lois being decapitated on the spot by a large, extremely sharp hatchet, but she ruthlessly shut down the picture. Revenge fantasies were not only out of place this morning, but unwarranted. All her best friend and her one-time-only lover had done was say hello.

"I assume it's okay if Lois keeps me company," she said, making sure to keep her voice a lot steadier than her insides. "I mean, stay here while I do the interview. Moral support."

"She can stay, but not in here. She'll have to sit in the booth. Can't take the chance of any accidental noise while we're on the air." Indicating the chair positioned in front of the second microphone, he said, "Grab a seat, Sarah, and I'll run over the setup with you. Lois?" He grinned again. "You see that glass wall there, with all the machines and junk behind it?"

"Sure do."

"Go out this door, turn right, and open the very next door. Marty, there, will make you comfortable. He's the engineer."

"Break a leg, Sarah," Lois said with a wink. "I'll be watching out for you."

After Lois walked out—with Tim checking out the rear view the entire time, Sarah observed—Tim turned to her. With a gesture that took in the whole glass-walled room, including a large console with hundreds of buttons, several machines and microphones, and the table and chairs, he said, "Welcome to my little world."

She was most definitely off-balance, Tim thought, which was good. She deserved it. He was angry at her—good and angry—even though he was determined not to show it. He would function smoothly and efficiently while dealing with her. And later, after the interview, he would hand her a paper bag and watch while she looked inside to see the garter belt and stockings she'd left outside his door last night. He would remain cool and composed the whole time.

Setting her purse on the table, Sarah gazed around, seeming confused. "Is Mr. Morrisey here?"

"No, he's not."

"He's not?"

Tim propped a hip against the edge of the console. She hadn't taken her seat yet; in fact, it was almost as though she were contemplating escape. "Don's running a little late, so I'm filling in for the first hour."

"Filling in?" she repeated.

"Yeah. Don't worry, you're in capable hands. I put in three years on talk radio in Seattle. Had quite a following, even if I do say so myself."

She clasped her hands nervously. "It isn't that. It's just… Well, I expected—"

"You expected Don Morrisey, and he's not here."

"Well, if Mr. Morrisey isn't here—" she picked up her purse and hugged it to her "—maybe we could make it another—"

"Scared, Sarah?" he interrupted, folding his arms across his chest. "Afraid I'll say or do something to embarrass you? Like talk about last night on the air?"

She nibbled at her lip. "Uh… Not really, no."

"Because I won't. I'm a professional and you're a professional, so there's no need to get into any of that."

"Well, it wasn't that, really, it's just—" She stopped, seemingly at a loss for words.

He felt powerful, in control. Glancing at his watch, he said, "Look, we have four minutes. We can keep doing this, or we can get down to business. What's your choice?"

He stared at her, forcing her to meet his gaze. When she did, he was sorry he had. She looked as though she'd just walked into a supposedly tame lion's den—not sure if she could trust her information, and not positive she could defend herself. Then she sank into the chair, playing with the clasp of her purse and, again, averting her gaze from his.

All of a sudden, that righteous anger he'd been feeling toward her began ebbing away. What was it about her that could heat up his temper and then reduce it to ashes in a split second when she revealed her vulnerability? Why couldn't he hold on to a little old-fashioned rage against the woman?

He had arranged for Don Morrisey to be late today by sending him out on a celebrity interview; Tim had planned to make Sarah squirm a bit on the air. Then she showed up, all in blue silk, her hair in a French braid, but wisps all over the place, looking distracted and off-balance. She even had a friend in tow.

And not a bad-looking friend, at that.

For all the good it did him. All he saw was Sarah, tired and ill at ease, and trying not to show it. The urge to comfort her—to take care of her, for God's sake!—was overwhelming.

*Put it away, Pelham,* he told himself. Knock off the compassion crap. Hold on to the anger but keep cool—it's your best defense.

He sat down in his chair, then leaned over and adjusted her mike. "We're going to do a sound check for level. Just talk, and Marty in there—" he pointed to the control room on the other side of the glass "—will adjust."

"What do I say?" Sarah asked.

"Anything you want. Just keep talking."

"Um—" Wide-eyed, she looked over at him and shrugged. "My mind is blank."

"Okay. How about those Giants?"

"The Giants?" she repeated. "Oh, yes. The baseball team."

"None other. What do you think of the new stadium?"

"Won't it be terribly expensive?"

"Sure will, but think of the revenue."

"I don't know, there's something about spending millions of dollars on new buildings when so many people are homeless—"

"Believe me, if it doesn't go to the stadium, it won't find its way to the homeless. Never has. Got it now, Marty?"

The engineer's voice came over the speaker. "Got it. Sarah, make sure you speak right into the center of the mike or you'll sound far away."

"All right," she said, obviously more comfortable now. "Tim, is the sound check over with?"

He found his earphones and adjusted a dial. "Uh-hmm."

"Then, what are we going to talk about? Is there a list of questions?"

"'The Don Morrisey Show' is unrehearsed talk radio, Sarah."

"I know, but, what if—?"

"Leave it to me," he said smoothly. "All you have to remember is this—with a live microphone in a studio, it's wise never to say anything you wouldn't want broadcast to the whole world."

Her hand flew to her mouth. "Oh, God."

"It's okay, we're not on the air yet." He glanced up at the large clock on the wall. "But we're about to be.

"Good morning," he said into the mike, his voice changing slightly into a warmer, more modulated sound. "We're here on 'The Don Morrisey Show' on KCAW, and this is Tim Pelham filling in for a short while. This morning our guest in the third hour will be Lonnie Coltrane, the recently fired aide to our esteemed mayor, who has a lot to say. In the second hour, Jimmie-Bob Bailey will tell us about going on the road with Willie Nelson in the good old days.

"Our guest in the first hour is Sarah Dann, owner-manager of an adult education school with a pretty provocative curriculum. If you browse through the catalog, you might see classes like 'How to Be a Dominatrix,' 'Learn to Please Your Husband in Bed' and 'An Overview of Pornography, the First Thousand Years.'

"First, though, listen to what a couple of our sponsors have to say, then we'll introduce you to Ms. Dann."

Tim said nothing for a beat, then Marty came over the speaker. "Clear."

Swiveling his chair so he faced Sarah, he smiled. "Okay, we're off for two minutes. Anything I can tell you?"

Sarah was furious. "What do you mean provocative?" She glared at the mike and tapped it gingerly. "Is this thing on?"

"Not right now. Hey, I saw a lot of stuff in your catalog that would raise eyebrows. Even your class Dating For Destiny. That's not a run-of-the-mill school course—or it wasn't in my day."

"But that kind of class is only a small percentage. We also offer college-level courses, remedial reading, job training—"

A buzz interrupted her sentence. "Save it for the air, okay, Sarah?" Tim pushed his headphones off and picked up the receiver on the nearby phone. "Yes?" He listened for a moment, then nodded. "All right. Tell him to make it eleven instead, and don't put any more calls through. I'm live on the air in about thirty seconds. Okay, honey."

When he hung up, Sarah asked, "Your secretary?"

"Yes."

"And you call her honey?"

"That's because her name is Honey. Honey Dotweiler."

"Oh." Damn him. He'd gotten her again.

And he knew it. He grinned, put his headphones in place again and spoke into the mike. "We're back on the air. Sarah Dann, say hello."

"Hello."

"We're going to be talking to Sarah for a while, so if you want to give us a call, KCAW's phones numbers are—"

While he read off a series of numbers, Sarah steeled herself to be ready for whatever came her way.

"Now Sarah, tell us all about Keep On Learning. Great name for a school, by the way. How'd you come up with it?"

"It's a quote from my sixth-grade teacher that always stuck with me. She ended each day with it: 'Stay open. Remain teachable. Keep on learning.'"

"Nice."

For the next few minutes, they talked about how Sarah had gone to work for the school after her divorce, then had become the manager, then the owner. She'd told this story often from the dais, and as it was familiar territory, she started to relax. Yes, she told herself, she could do this. In fact, being on the radio was okay. So far.

"Tell us about the class entitled Dating For Destiny," Tim suggested. "By the way, folks, it's quite an experience. I know, I took it. It's informative and lots of fun."

"Well, thanks, Tim."

"Tell us, Sarah. How did you come up with the idea?"

Even this question was one for which she was prepared; she spoke of the changing, shrinking world, the women's movement and the shift in courtship rituals, the electronic explosion. She finished by saying, "It just seemed there was a need, so I tried to fill it."

"You know, when I first walked into your classroom and saw all those single people, I had the impression that someone could use your class as a kind of pickup place."

She felt the hairs on the back of her neck bristle a warning. "Not really," she said conversationally, then chuckled good-naturedly. "Or not intentionally, anyway. It costs money to enroll, and while you're there, it requires real work and paying attention. I think it's more like attending a work-related seminar. If you meet someone, great, but that isn't the purpose."

"I see. Then how do you feel about casual sex?"

"Excuse me?"

"Casual sex."

"I heard you. I just wasn't sure how that connected to what we were just talking about."

"Oh. I meant, what do you tell your class about one-nighters—unemotional, recreational involvements? I'm curious, and I'll bet a lot of our listeners would like to know, Sarah."

"Really?"

"I'm sure of it."

"I don't tell them anything, Tim. I'm not anyone's mother." She heard the edge in her voice, so she smoothed it out. "That kind of thing is a personal choice, isn't it? Or it should be."

"All right, then. How do you feel about it *personally*, Sarah?"

She could feel her teeth grinding. The interview had stopped being enjoyable. The son of a bitch. "I discourage it, *Tim*, for health reasons, if nothing more. Also, it seems to me that if you have a series of impersonal encounters, it might be difficult to make the transition to more personal ones." She paused. "Something along the lines of—if someone continues to exercise one muscle only, the others get out of shape. Emotionally speaking, of course," she added.

"Of course." Grinning, he gave her the thumbs-up sign.

So, he admired her comeback, did he? There was more where that came from. The uncertainty, the passivity she'd been feeling since last night was gone, gone, gone.

"So," Tim continued, "in the absence of a deep commitment, you encourage abstinence, is that it?"

"I encourage nothing except to be true to yourself and your nature."

"Well put. Tell me this, then, Sarah. Do you think it's honestly possible, in today's world, to believe in romance? In the possibility of long-lasting, faithful love? Ponder that one, won't you, while we take a break."

"Clear," Marty said.

"Don't, Tim," Sarah warned.

"Don't what?"

"You're playing with me. And I don't care for it."

"Are you kidding? I'm interviewing you. And you're doing great."

Keeping her voice as low as possible, she said, "You're paying me back for last night. You said you wouldn't."

"Shh. Remember we're live."

"No, we're not. Marty said we're clear."

"But he can hear us, can't you, Marty? And Lois, too."

Looking up, Sarah saw two grinning heads nodding behind the glass partition. She put her hand over the mike. "I'll get you, I swear I will," she hissed.

"I look forward to it."

Tim made sure to hide his chuckle as he swiveled his chair back around. Sarah on the offensive was a wonder to behold. "We're back," he said into the mike, "and I've asked Sarah if she believes in love. What's your answer?"

"Let me turn that around. Do you believe in love?"

"I'm not being interviewed."

"Humor me...or are you afraid of the question?"

He scratched his head. "You know, I'm not sure what I feel about it. How's that for an answer?"

"It's honest...and just about what I expected. I go in and out on it myself. Which brings me to one of our most popular courses—Decision Making in the Nineties. It's taught by a world-famous psychologist, Dr. Joanna George, author of the book..."

Tim kept the interview in neutral territory for a while, then he took some phone calls from listeners. Many of them came from those curious about the more sexually suggestive classes, but Sarah skewed her answers cleverly, so that she could promote other, more run-of-the-mill courses of interest.

She handled herself well, he had to admit, her ease with language and natural sense of humor making her a fine guest. After the next break, Tim said, "We have time for a couple more calls. And by the way, I want to put in a personal plug for Keep On Learning. What's the number our listeners can call for the free catalog, Sarah?"

She recited the number, but watched him closely, as though wondering if he was going to pull something. He grinned. He felt a lot better when she was willing to do battle than when she looked lost.

A twentyish-sounding woman named Fern was the last caller. "I think your class about dating is a big hype," she declared in a high-pitched, accusatory tone of voice. "It's just a way to make money, like those psychic networks and personal ads. No one ever actually meets anyone that way, I'm sure of it."

"As a matter of fact—" Sarah began, but Tim cut her off.

"Fern? I want to repeat that I took the Dating For Destiny class, and it sure worked for me. I've had a *wonderful* time putting all of Sarah's suggestions into use."

"Thank you, Tim," Sarah said graciously. "Fern, we offer a follow-up program, where we match people who took the class at different times. The fee is pretty reasonable, and there have been successful matchups, I promise."

"That's right," Tim added. "Through Sarah and her class, I've met all kinds of new, extremely interesting women."

"See, Fern? It can be done."

"Meeting people is one thing," Fern complained. "Have you met your mate?"

Sarah looked at him. "Have you, Tim? I'm sure the listeners would love to hear all about it."

"Well, no, I haven't found that special one yet, the one that would make me give up my bachelor ways." He chuckled. "But I'm still looking."

"I thought so," Fern said smugly.

"Don't go by Tim's experience only," Sarah cautioned. "He's pretty confirmed in his ways—not a great candidate for all the hard work and willingness to change that's required in a love relationship. But, as I said, there have been successes. As a matter of fact, Tim was at a wedding yesterday, weren't you, Tim? And I've attended eleven others, where the bride and groom met, one way or another, through my class."

"Really?" Fern asked, sounding less sure of herself now, and hopeful, too.

"Really. Come on down to the school and you can thumb through our wedding scrapbook. Lots of happy graduates in there."

"Wow."

"It's not easy, though, as I always tell my class. You have to keep shopping, keep trying. So, what do you think

Tim? We'll be glad to arrange another list of eligible women. How does that sound?''

"Hey, if I'm such a hard case," he grumbled, "why even bother?"

"You're kind of a challenge, I guess."

"Am I? Oh, well, thanks, Sarah, but I don't think so."

"Why?" Both Sarah and Fern asked the question at the same time.

"Well…"

"What's the matter, Tim?" Sarah asked. "Discouraged? Giving up after—what? Three dates?"

"Yeah." Fern was now aggressively on Sarah's side. "You can't give up so quickly."

"So, Tim, how about it? Ready for another list of five women from Keep On Learning?"

"Say yes," Fern urged. "And I want to know what happens."

"Terrific idea," Sarah agreed enthusiastically. "Why don't you give the listeners a progress report?"

"Because this isn't my show," he said pointedly. How had he let the direction of the interview get away from him? "I'm just the subst—"

Sarah cut in smoothly. "I'm sure Don Morrisey won't mind. Besides, aren't you the manager of KCAW? Don't tell me you can't arrange for a little airtime for yourself. Help me out here, Fern."

"Yeah. A challenge. He can give a progress report. And, incidentally—" she sounded coy now "—I wouldn't mind being one of the five on your list."

Sarah grinned. "Come on down to the school and ask for me personally, okay, Fern? I'll see what we can do. Now, calling and arranging dates with five women may take a little time. How about a progress report, say, three weeks from today? Tim, after your generosity in giving me airtime this morning, it's the least I can do for you. Are you game?''

He looked daggers at her, but he really didn't have a choice. ''Gee, Sarah, I can't wait.''

# 10

———◄———

"Listen," Tim said, when Marty gave them the "clear" sign. "That was pushing it a little far, wasn't it?"

On a high, Sarah wanted to grin, but she merely lifted an eyebrow. "Think so?"

"Hey, Timbo! Give me back my show!"

Sarah assumed the curly-haired man who shot into the studio, all hyperenergized, his face wreathed in a broad smile, was Don Morrisey.

"Got a great interview—Shelly Diaz is a dish. Thanks for subbing. Hi," he said to Sarah. "Sorry, got to toss you both out of here now." He swiped the earphones from Tim and stood behind him, his foot tapping restlessly. "We got this phone patch to set up."

Tim scrambled up from the chair. "Sure, Don. Sorry. Coming, Sarah?"

She picked up her purse and preceded Tim out the door. When they were in the corridor, he looked both ways, as though making sure no one was in earshot.

"What I meant was," he said, "did you have to do that bit about the list? I don't want any part of a corny challenge. I'm not an on-air personality, I'm a manager."

"Not dignified enough for you?" She shrugged. "Then don't do it. It makes no difference to me."

Scratching his head, he glared at her. It was obvious he was both pissed off and baffled by her.

She felt herself softening. In the last part of the interview, she'd certainly gotten even with him for his jabs at her; it was time to stop the swordplay. "Tim—listen," she said reasonably. "I got a little carried away. Whatever you want to do about it, just let me know, all right?"

When he didn't reply, she looked toward the control room, but Lois didn't seem in a hurry to come out. Sarah's mood was no longer upbeat, and she wanted out of here.

Shifting her purse onto her shoulder, she said, "I really want to thank you for the opportunity to be on the show. It was invaluable publicity for the school. And, well—" now she felt a little embarrassed "—I think it went rather well. Do you? I mean, compared with other interviews?" She was blatantly fishing for a compliment, she thought. She should be ashamed of herself.

"Yeah, it was fine." Propping a shoulder against the wall, Tim looked down at his feet and shook his head.

A perky redhead walked by, holding a large cylindrical container. "Hi, Tim."

He looked up. "Hi, Rosalie."

"The numbers are in for last month," she said, continuing to hurry down the corridor. "They're on your desk."

"Thanks." Meeting Sarah's gaze, Tim shook his head again. "What am I going to do with you?"

"Do with me?"

Moving away from the wall, he planted his feet firmly. "Okay, do you want to talk about last night? You mentioned something about it, remember? That I was paying you back?" He dug his hands into his pockets, obviously ill at ease. "I'm willing to talk about it if you are. In my office, if you'd like. Or we could grab a cup of coffee."

She wasn't prepared—not now, not with Lois along and in the middle of the morning, and before she'd gathered her thoughts and knew exactly how she did feel about last night.

But he'd brought it up, which was gutsy of him, and she owed him something. She couldn't back away; not completely, anyhow.

Sarah stood for a moment, playing with the clasp of her purse. Finally, she said slowly, "I...wanted to apologize for my behavior. It was...pretty irrational, and some of the stuff I said to you was unfair."

He emitted a relieved breath. "Oh. Yeah, well, I guess I said some things, too."

"We both did."

"So—" He was more relaxed now; she could tell from his posture. "Can we talk about it?"

"We just did. We apologized."

"And that's it? No discussion?"

"What is there to discuss?" She was starting to get that backed-against-the-wall feeling, and she didn't like it.

"What is there to discuss?" he repeated. "What? We're to just pretend it never happened, is that it?"

An older man with a white beard came out of a nearby studio. "Lovely morning, isn't it?" he said in a beautiful, resonant, actor's speaking voice as he passed them.

"Couldn't be lovelier, Ernie," Tim replied, then eyed Sarah again. "You didn't answer my question."

"Maybe it's for the best."

Folding his arms across his chest, he challenged, "Which part do we forget about? The fight? Or—" his voice softened "—what went before the fight?"

Her skin heated instantly at the memory of the two of them, thrashing about on the huge white couch, their gasps and cries and sighs punctuating the furious movements of two aching bodies, desperate to be joined. As her pulse rate quickened, she felt herself sinking once again into powerlessness in Tim's presence. She needed to put a stop to that, and now.

"Both. After and before." Swallowing down her shakiness, she offered her hand and said crisply, "Well, thanks again for the chance to talk up the school. Do you want another list, or not?"

He stared at her hand, a frown between his brows. Then he shrugged, but he didn't return the handshake. "Whatever—who cares? Sure. Fax me another list."

"All right. These women will be less obviously glamorous, I think. There's not as much chance for...eccentricities."

The control room door opened and Lois walked out, laughing as she waved in Marty's direction. "Great jokes!" she called out to the engineer. "Thanks. Bye, now. I had a blast." To Sarah, she said, "Hey, you were great!"

Then she turned toward Tim. "Wasn't she?"

"Great."

Lois smiled slyly. "What *did* happen last night, hmm?"

Tim answered the question, but kept his gaze on Sarah as he did. "Apparently, nothing."

"Oh?" Lois looked from her friend to Tim and back again. Then she said, "Ah, well," and grabbed Sarah's arm. "I've simply got to get back home before I collapse right here. C'mon."

Tim drummed his fingers on the steering wheel and, one more time, checked out the nursery school entrance. The building was obviously a converted residence, and was brightly painted with scenes of cloud-filled skies and trees. His was one of a line of cars in front of the school, the others mostly station wagons and sturdy Volvos, with stickers on their fenders proclaiming someone's son as an honor student at a school, or offering to sell Girl Scout cookies.

He felt a little out of place in all this family-values type atmosphere, but it went with the territory of nursery-school teacher, he supposed, which was the profession of Wendy

Milman, number one on list number two, also known as the fifth woman he'd contacted.

The fifth woman, that is, if he didn't count Sarah. And he didn't.

Tim fidgeted some more. He'd only been waiting for a few minutes, but he had this really strong urge to take off. The only reason he was even here was because he wouldn't let Sarah think he'd turned down a challenge.

Sarah again.

He'd always thought of himself as an easygoing, fairly calm person; it took a lot to make him lose his temper. But in the three days since he'd seen Sarah at the station, he'd done nothing but snap at his co-workers, make surly remarks at Sully's, and talk back to the idiots on TV. This was new behavior, and he didn't care for it—not in the least.

It was all Sarah's fault. Sarah and her stupid challenge.

No! He shut the subject off with a mental door slam. He would *not* think about her. Eventually, she would vacate his brain. And good riddance to her.

A bell sounded, and the pink- and blue-striped door flew open with a bang. A crowd of kids came running and jumping outside. As each saw their moms or dads, they ran toward them with arms wide and huge grins.

Open arms. He'd had nothing like this when he was a kid. Nursery school? No one in his family had ever heard of it. Grade school was hit and miss, depending on his father's post and state of inebriation.

But he'd gotten through it, hadn't he? And relatively unscarred, comparatively speaking.

He noticed a curly-headed little girl standing to the side, her index finger in her mouth, and an anxious expression on her face. Her worried gaze searched up and down the street, as though she was afraid no one was coming for her.

Something about her expression got to him. Concern

made him look up the street and into his rearview mirror. A sudden lump formed in his throat. He wanted to jump out of the car and comfort her, to tell her it would be all right.

He felt the anger building again. What kind of idiot parents did she have, that no one was there to pick her up? There ought to be a test before you were allowed to procreate—

Just then, a huge smile changed the child's face from the picture of anxiety to one of pure joy. "Papa!" she cried, and ran up to a large, bearded man. After he'd hugged her and whirled her around, he sat her on his shoulders and took her for a little gallop. She giggled and held on tight to his hair. He winced, but didn't seem to mind at all.

Thank God she was safe, Tim thought, taken aback by the strong rush of emotion he'd just felt. An innocent child, so trusting, so at the mercy of the grown-ups. Kids should be loved and should never be let down, he thought. It was their right. Man, if he ever had a kid—

"Whoa," Tim said aloud. How'd he gotten started on this little tangent? Him with a kid? To take care of and love and give all the things grown-ups are supposed to give to children? He would have no idea what to do—not in the least.

Frowning, he stared straight ahead. Why was he thinking this way? He'd never even entertained a thought like this, except in passing. And never seriously. It must have been that little girl and the look on her face.

Or maybe it was Sarah.

The other night, when she'd passionately told him about the family she wanted—the kids, the home, the husband— there had been such yearning in her face, such a strong need. He remembered feeling both uncomfortable and vaguely guilty at the time, because he knew he wasn't up to filling that need.

So...Sarah was responsible for him thinking about kids. Damn her.

His musings were interrupted when a small woman came out of the kindergarten door, surrounded by a circle of more clamoring five-year-olds. This was Wendy Milman of the Sunshine and Stars Nursery School. She appeared—in her short-sleeved white T-shirt and girlish jumper—to have a nice enough body. Her hair was soft brown with hints of gold, and she wore small, round, tortoiseshell glasses, which gave her an owlish look.

Tim studied the scene. Wendy seemed to have a nice rapport with those kids, which meant her nature was probably loving and warm, the direct opposite of his usual pleasure-seeking ladies.

He still would rather not be here, but he would give it the old college try. Maybe they would go for a late-afternoon cup of coffee, or a stroll down on the docks. He would ask her what she'd like to do, and they would take it from there.

Tim got out of his car but remained standing on the driver's side, leaning an elbow casually on the top of the open door. "If you're not Wendy," he said with a grin, "you have one extremely large family."

Several children clung to her skirt and two tugged at her sleeve, but the woman glanced up at the sound of his comment. "Pardon?" Her voice was high and soft. "Oh, yes," she said after a beat. "You're kidding, aren't you? Ha-ha."

This last sentence was delivered in a singsong rhythm, as though she was used to reading nursery tales and couldn't quite turn it off. Funny, he hadn't noticed that particular quality when they'd spoken on the phone.

After closing his car door, he strolled around to the passenger side and offered his hand. "Tim Pelham."

Nodding, she smiled sweetly. "I kind of figured.

Tina—'' she addressed a tiny, dark-skinned child ''—if you let go, I can shake the nice man's hand.''

Tina let go, Wendy shook his hand with her much smaller one, and Tim felt and smelled a layer of peanut butter on his palm. He looked down at it in horror.

''Oh, my. Tina,'' Wendy said patiently, ''we're supposed to wash our hands after snack time, aren't we?''

''Yeth. But Donny thtole the thoap.''

''How awful. Donny's already gone. Well, we'll bring it up at Grouch Period tomorrow, shall we?'' She looked up at Tim and wrinkled her nose. ''Will you be all right?''

''Sure,'' he said, wiping his hand on the back of his new twill pants. Why was he here? Why had he agreed to this?

Wendy turned to the few children still in the yard, now supervised by an efficient-looking young woman. ''Behave for Belinda, children. Goodbye, silly heads!''

''Goodbye, Miss Milman,'' they said, except for one child, who shouted out, ''You're a poo-poo head.''

''Jason?'' Wendy placed her small hands on her narrow hips and looked stern. ''What did I say about using that expression?''

Jason, a roly-poly towhead, looked down at his feet and stuck his bottom lip out. ''Not nice.''

''And we always want to be nice, don't we?''

He nodded.

''Because nice behavior makes nice people.''

''Yes, Miss Milman.''

''All right, then. I'll see you all tomorrow,'' she sang out.

''See you tomorrow,'' came back the chorus of young voices. The whole thing was reminiscent of *The Sound of Music;* Tim half expected the children to erupt in ''So Long, Farewell.''

Again, Wendy gazed up at Tim, smiled and wrinkled her nose. He didn't know if he could take being in the presence of someone who did that all the time. It made her look like a nearsighted mouse.

He helped her into her seat, then walked around to the driver's side.

He would try, he thought, he would really try.

If he ever saw Sarah again, he would wring her neck.

"Yes, Fern, I passed it on. Now it's up to him...."

Sarah rubbed her eyes, not even caring about the mascara. It had been a really long day—lots of meetings, phone calls, scheduling, making nice with agents, hanging tough with hotel banquet room bookers. It was five o'clock and she was barely able to remain patient as she listened to Fern's haranguing.

"No, I can't force him to call you," Sarah said, "because that's not how it's done.... Yes, I know you're signed up for the class, but that's not till next week, so in the meantime, you'll just have to be patient.... Yes, I appreciate all the friends you've recommended to us, really I do.... All right, I'll try. I don't guarantee anything, but I'll try."

She hung up, wanting to whimper with exasperation. Fern, her on-air ally, had turned into a royal pain. She'd become fixated on meeting Tim, and felt it was her right to do so.

Sarah checked the small print on a contract that she'd been studying when Fern had called. Her eyes refused to focus, even with the reading glasses.

She sat back in her chair and rotated her neck. Tight? You bet. Her glance fell on the phone, and she debated what to do. She'd promised Fern to call Tim and request he call her. What Sarah had wanted to do was get rid of the woman, but she'd promised.

And Sarah wanted to talk to Tim—wanted it badly.

Her hand actually itched with wanting to pick up the phone and hold it to her ear while she punched in KCAW's number. For the past two days, she'd grabbed the receiver, replaced it, grabbed it and replaced it, like some constant dieter trying not to snatch one of an inviting plateful of chocolate chip cookies.

She really ought to call him, she told herself, to find out how the current list was working out.

Liar.

She wanted to hear his voice.

She would not call him....

Although she should. She'd promised Fern.

She could lie to Fern and say she had.

But Sarah really wanted to call him.

The thing was, she couldn't make Tim vanish from her thoughts.

From more than her thoughts. Lower down, her body kept remembering again and again how it had felt that one night they'd been together—the depth of her arousal, the sensation of male muscle and sinew under her fingertips and the feel of his hands driving her wild; the pervasive heat all through her bones and skin and bloodstream; the final explosion that had felt like nothing in her experience, that had shocked her to the very core of her being.

Memories of that night came rushing back to her at the oddest times—in her bath, while sipping her morning coffee, in her office during the day.

Yesterday, in fact, she'd been in the middle of an extremely important breakfast meeting at the Sir Francis Drake Hotel. An ex-senator had written a tell-all about Washington, and Sarah wanted to sign him up for a one-time lecture. Somewhere between the orange juice and the presentation of the bill, she'd drifted off into replaying highlights of her and Tim's lovemaking, and had registered nothing of the senator's conversation. Thank heaven he'd been long-winded and fond of his own voice; she doubted he'd even noticed her inattention. She sincerely hoped she hadn't said or promised anything too extreme.

Tim was definitely a distraction. But what was she to do about it? She was hopeless, she supposed; absolutely hopeless. Doomed to a life of lusting after someone who wasn't any more capable of change than she was.

People didn't change their basic natures; that was a lesson she'd learned very young. Her parents had been rigid and had remained so until they died. Her husband had been the same, although he'd been nicer about it. Sarah herself hadn't changed a lot. She might appear to be a capable, mature woman now, but underneath she was still shy, still troubled by decision making, still engaged in a constant war between her emotional nature and reason.

No, people didn't change; they became even more what they were when they were first formed.

Commitment had always been just out of Tim's reach and would remain so.

As he would remain just out of hers.

Still, she ought to call....

Just as she reached for the receiver one more time, the phone rang, making her jump in her chair. Could it be one of those moments when the vibes between two people were so strong, all she had to do was think about him and he called?

She waited for Marianne to pick up, but on the fourth ring, she did it herself. "Sarah Dann."

"Hello? Sarah? It's David."

Her heart deflated as quickly as a pool float ready to be stored for winter. "Oh, hello, David."

David was someone she'd met on a plane a couple of months previously. He traveled most of the time, and whenever he was in town, he called to ask her out. She always politely refused, but, good-naturedly, he kept coming back.

"You sound far away," she said.

"I'm on a plane, winging my way back from Paraguay. And in my briefcase are two tickets to Beethoven's Ninth, conducted by Zubin Mehta, this Saturday. I really think it's time you went out with me. We could have dinner before. Don't say no."

"I'm sorry—"

Sarah stopped herself. Why not? Why not go out on a real date? Let someone into her life—someone eligible, well-groomed, polite, a classical music lover. She'd been wallowing in self-pity, acting almost pathological about this "no men" thing.

Except for Tim, of course. And he didn't count.

It was time. More than seven months had passed, and she was over her broken heart about Charles. She was unattached and available. She was, in fact, a free woman.

Besides, she loved the Ninth, with its magnificent choral last movement. "All right, David. I'd love to."

After they arranged times and meeting places and she hung up the phone, she wondered why she didn't feel more upbeat. She'd crossed a line, hadn't she? Decided to officially—Tim didn't count—get into the dating thing again.

She wanted to find her destiny.

She taught a class in the subject, for heaven's sake! It was time the teacher put the lessons to use.

She pressed her intercom button. "Marianne, please look in the Dating For Destiny follow-up file, and bring in the folder marked Males: Ages Thirty to Forty-five. Thanks."

While she waited, her fingers drumming restlessly on the desktop, Sarah tried to rev herself up for Saturday evening. In truth, she wanted to spend several hours with David as much as she wanted to do her laundry.

Damn. She probably had to clear up this ridiculous situation with Tim first.

The challenge—she could talk to him about the challenge, maybe let him off the hook. They'd been live on the air, so she'd given him no option. That hadn't been really honorable of her.

Yes, she assured herself. She needed to call Tim.

With crisp determination, she called the radio station and asked to be put through to him.

He wasn't there, she was told. Would she like to leave a message on his voice mail? Yes, she would.

"Tim? It's Sarah Dann. Uh, how are you? I'm calling to…find out if the new list is working out better than the old one." No, she wasn't. "Well, not really, but, I guess I don't want to… I mean, not over the phone. You know."

This was not the way she'd intended to sound. She scrambled desperately for something more to say, knowing she was being mercilessly recorded, and there was no way she could play it back and delete the stupid parts.

"Oh, yes." She thought of something else to say. "Thanks again for the help with promotion. We've had over three hundred calls for our catalog, and registration is up about twelve percent. So, again, thanks. Um, I guess that's all. There's no need to call back unless you'd like to."

After she hung up, she placed her head in her hands and groaned. Why had she said that last bit about not needing to call back? It sounded like a come-on.

But she *wanted* him to call back.

No, she didn't.

"Both of you, shut up." She said this aloud just as Marianne walked into her office, holding a full manila file folder.

Her secretary gazed around the room. "Who were you just speaking to?"

"Myself."

"But you said, 'Both of you.'"

"I'm a Gemini," Sarah grumbled. "Sue me."

Marianne set the papers down on her desk and, shaking

her head over her employer's strange behavior, returned to the outer office.

Sarah grabbed the folder and attacked it with a vengeance.

"Enough," she muttered.

Enough time spent on Tim Pelham. He either would or would not call back. It was nothing to her. Nothing at all.

## 11

Number two on list number two hadn't returned Tim's call. So, it was on to number three, Nora Calhoun. Tim had decided this was the last one. End of discussion. He'd had enough.

Sarah had left word on his voice mail—she'd wanted to find out how it was going. He hadn't returned her call. He was still angry, and still wishing the old, calm and smiling Tim would put in an appearance, so he could feel like a human being again.

Nora had suggested the two of them meet at an art gallery featuring the works of an artist with an unpronounceable Eastern European name, lots of Ys and Zs and no vowels. The artist was obviously pretty troubled—all around the high-ceilinged room were hung massive oil paintings filled with pain. There were cowering bodies, lots of blood-red splashes and other vivid colors, black-robed and hooded figures, deformed bodies, skulls, knives.

Tim shuddered as he gazed at yet another scene of carnage. He understood that the artist's part of the world had a bloody, savage history. He even understood that all art represented one person's vision, or experience, or imagination, or whatever.

But this art sure wasn't Tim's kind of thing.

Nora Calhoun, with one arm across her middle supporting the other elbow, and her fingers stroking her chin, gazed fixedly at one of these paintings. While she studied it, Tim studied her.

Nora was a highly regarded prosecuting attorney in the D.A.'s office. When he'd called, she'd invited him to meet her here in North Beach, at a friend's opening. She'd described herself as Morticia Addams with short hair. At the time he'd thought, Good, a woman with a sense of humor.

But she hadn't been kidding.

Nora was rail thin, dressed all in black, her hair cut very short, so the fine, sharp bones of her face were prominent. She wore black eyeliner and pale lipstick, and her face was as near to white—powder, he assumed—as to almost appear clownlike.

"Interesting use of grisaille, don't you think?" she said, turning to him.

"What is grisaille?" Tim asked. "I have to admit I'm not real familiar with the terminology."

"You're not?" She raised an eyebrow. "I was very specific about being an art lover on that form I filled out. Very specific. I expected you would be one, too."

He tried to shrug off the feeling of being attacked, of being judged and found wanting, somehow.

"I see it this way," he said casually. "You know some things well, I know some things well. People can't have everything in common, can they? Then, except for anatomy, it'd be like being with a clone of yourself. There'd be nothing to teach each other."

Her eyes narrowed as she seemed to think this over. Then she nodded approvingly. "Good point. Differences are important, I give you that. Except I really love art. I'm at a gallery or a museum three or four times a week."

"And I'm at a game or at a bar watching a game the same amount of time."

"Sports?"

"Uh-huh."

"Hmm. Interesting. I've just begun to watch European soccer lately, on cable. It's quite fascinating."

"It sure is." Soccer? Oh, well. It was a start.

But he wished her body were a little more rounded. And her hair a little less black—maybe more on the reddish side.

He wished she were Sarah.

As they moved on to the next painting, he gave himself a silent talking-to. Remember? He'd wondered about guys enslaved by their attachment to a woman. He was becoming a prime example. He'd never thought he was a masochist, but he was sure acting like one. More punishment, give me more. Use me, hurt me.

Suddenly, some of the paintings didn't seem so off base, after all.

It had to stop, he told himself firmly. It really did. He would put an end to it, right away. Cut off all communication with her, wipe her out of his mind.

He reminded himself that he'd been saying something along the same lines all week, and had done nothing about it.

But this time he meant it.

"Can I get you a glass of champagne?" he asked Nora.

She smiled at him; it was stiff, as though her mouth wasn't used to lifting at the corners, but it was a smile. "That would be very nice. Thank you."

"Maybe some cheese and crackers, too? I haven't eaten dinner, have you?"

"No, thanks. I never eat dinner."

"Never?"

"Never. I have one meal in the morning, after my work-out. It's how I keep my shape." She stroked one hand down her side, over her barely discernible hipline.

It was his cue to compliment her on her thinness, but he couldn't. She didn't have anything close to what he called a shape. Sure, Nora was probably exactly what the women's magazines pronounced as perfect, but to him she was a long pole with a few minor bumps thrown in along the way.

And so damned pale. Did she even have blood running through her veins? Or was it embalming fluid?

Face it, he told himself. She just wasn't his type. But just what *was* his "type" he didn't know. He used to know, but his world had become hopelessly scrambled in the past few weeks. He no longer knew who he was or what he felt. About a lot of things.

Two mind-numbing hours later—hours filled with small talk that sounded either pretentious or too art-world specific for him to understand—he thanked Nora for the invitation and beat it out of there.

He got into his car, put in a reggae CD, cranked up the volume and decided to air his brain out. He would treat himself to a long drive, let the car take him where it wanted to go.

He wasn't really surprised when it wound up in Sarah's neighborhood. Lowering the volume on his sound system, he turned onto her street, wondering if she was home on a Saturday night.

If she was, he would follow through on his decision to end it. He needed what the resident KCAW on-air psychologist referred to as "closure." And he needed it tonight.

As Tim drove by her house, he saw her standing at her front door. Slowing down as he passed, he was able to make out that she wore something long and formal looking, with a shimmering silver thing around her bare shoulders. Her hair was upswept and something shiny dangled from her ears. Her outfit screamed pure class.

Tim couldn't help but notice that Sarah was not alone on her front porch. She was with another person, and that person was a man. Only the back of this man was visible, but he appeared to be tall and dressed in a gray suit.

They stood very close together under the yellow porch light.

A jolt of jealousy shot through him like a cannon, and he actually bit down hard enough on his bottom lip to draw blood. In the space of five seconds, he imagined grabbing the guy and tossing him under a passing car, then carrying Sarah off to some cave, dumping her on the floor, and showing her, repeatedly, what she was missing when she even entertained the thought of other men. In this fantasy, of course, she loved every minute of her "lesson."

By now, he was at the end of her block. He ordered himself to drive on, to get himself home or to Sully's, ASAP.

But his car disagreed. As though Tim had no say in it, the vehicle turned right, then right again, and came around to Sarah's street once more.

Sarah sighed, but kept her voice as even as possible. "I'm sorry, David, it's a little late."

"C'mon. Jus' one little drink."

"You've already had several, and they weren't little."

"But Sarah—" her name came out sounding more like Shara "—all this time we've been friends." He was whining now, and she gritted her teeth. She hated whining, especially from men. "I jus' wanna come in. Sit for a while."

"I don't think so."

One of his arms rose, as though it were attached to a puppet string, and rested on the door frame. He leaned in her general direction and fell against her, pinning her to the door. His breath smelled like the alleyway behind a distillery.

She averted her head so she wouldn't pass out from the

stench. A perfect end to an awful evening. Really annoyed now, Sarah pushed at him. "David, move off me. Now."

"How 'bout a little kiss, Sarah. Jus' one."

Nearby, a newcomer announced his presence with a cough, followed by, "Is there a problem?"

Sarah was startled at the sound of Tim's voice. What was he doing here? And thank heavens he was. "Tim!" she said with desperate cheer. "Hi."

He stood just behind David, one foot resting on the upper of the two steps of her porch while the other stayed at ground level. He was dressed casually in dark slacks and a pale green long-sleeved cashmere sweater. She thought he looked about as good as a man could look.

"Who's your friend?" he asked.

David swayed toward her again and even though his eyes were closed, he seemed not so much to be making a pass as looking for someone or something to hold him up. Sarah pushed him away and Tim caught him before he fell all the way back.

"Huh?" David opened his eyes.

"Tim Pelham," Sarah said, "meet David Galway. David and I just went to hear Beethoven. It was a wonderful concert."

"That's nice," Tim observed. "An all-you-can-drink-type affair, was it?"

Sarah studied him for a moment. He was steely-eyed, but trying for humor. Some emotion seethed just below the surface, however, and it came to her with a flash of recognition.

He was jealous!

She felt a flutter of excitement in her chest. His jealousy was not only flattering, but it meant he must still care for her. A little, anyway. And she liked that he was jealous, because it made her spurts of the same emotion seem less irrational.

Smiling, she said, "The concert wasn't where the problem began. It was the bar we went to afterward. Bars, I should say. David knows every single one of them in downtown San Francisco."

David, still weaving, frowned and tried to focus on Tim. "Two lousy glasses of wine, thass all she had. What's the matter with the woman?"

"You got me there," Tim replied.

"And now she won't invite me in," he continued, as though he'd found a sympathetic ear. "Can you believe it?"

He listed to one side, and Tim propped him up against the porch post, holding him with one hand splayed across the other man's chest. "Where's his car?" he asked Sarah.

"Over there." She pointed to a large new American sedan parked in her driveway. "I drove us here from the last stop. It seemed the smart thing to do."

"Why don't you go in and call a cab?"

"Hey, what…?" David began, then seemed to lose his train of thought.

"I'll entertain the music lover, Sarah."

It was sound advice, so she took it, humming a little to herself all the while. Once she got inside, she leaned against her door and closed her eyes, barely able to contain the soaring sense of happiness she felt. Tim was here! And she'd thought she would never see him again.

He hadn't called her back after her voice-mail message to him earlier in the week, so she'd tried to resign herself to the fact that their last meeting had been their final one.

Just yesterday, she'd taken out the Dating For Destiny follow-up files again and scanned the pictures and fact sheets of several absolutely appropriate men. There were lawyers, doctors, businessmen, college professors; men with season's tickets to the ballet, men who either had or wanted kids, who believed in commitment and fidelity, who considered themselves evolved enough to actually talk about feelings....

She'd tried, really she had, to work up some enthusiasm. In the past, all of these qualities would have been high priorities for her. But none of them, not one, had even scratched the surface of her interest.

With her head in her hands as she'd sat at her desk, she faced herself as squarely as possible. All of this furious activity, this resolve to date, this list of eligible men—it was all hogwash. It was time to stop lying to herself, she'd realized. The man she wanted was Tim; he wasn't on the list because she kept refusing to put him there.

Tonight, that very man was on the premises, on her porch. He'd come to see her, and was jealous of David. And the evening, which had started out so badly, was now overflowing with possibilities.

After making her call, Sarah opened the screen door and stepped outside. Tim and David were seated on the top step, David with his head resting against the post, snoring loudly, while Tim stared out at the night.

"I'll wait with him, Sarah," he said, without looking at her.

How good he was to her, how kind. "You don't have to."

"It's okay. Just don't go to sleep yet." He turned his head and met her gaze. "I want to talk to you."

More chest flutters greeted this statement, and she smiled self-consciously. "Well, then, I'll change clothes and be right out."

He seemed so *serious,* Sarah thought with a small shiver of anticipation. What did he want to discuss with her? She couldn't wait to find out.

After removing her evening clothes, she put on a pair of jeans and a long sweater. As she looked in the mirror, she had the same reaction she'd had earlier in the evening while dressing to meet David. Somehow, she'd become thinner. By several pounds.

How had that happened? she wondered. True, she hadn't been eating much, not since she'd met Tim; or remet Tim, to be completely accurate. But that behavior was so unlike her—to eat less but not on purpose, to lose weight and not notice it. Usually, when she was upset, she gorged her way through it, then had to deprive herself for weeks afterward to get back to a decent weight. This was the first time she could remember *forgetting* to eat.

She supposed she'd been thinking—or not thinking—about other things for these past weeks. She'd been off-the-wall, to be honest.

Interesting thought. Maybe she ought to work on being upset, sexually turned-on, terrified, distracted, happy, angry and sad, on a regular basis. She would never have another weight problem in her life.

She grinned at the thought, then hurried outside to be with Tim again.

David was gone when she got there, and Tim was coming up her walk, holding a small Gump's shopping bag in his hand. A gift? For her?

She sat down on one side of the top step and Tim sank down next to her, setting the bag by his feet and keeping some distance between himself and her. He propped a shoulder on the post, with the opposite elbow resting against one bent knee.

The chest flutters had spread to her stomach. Had he been reevaluating their relationship, too? Was that why he was here? What did he want to bring up?

And, this time, what would she say?

"So," she offered, with a shaky but encouraging smile.

"So," he offered back, nodding briefly.

Tim had no idea how to do this. He focused his attention on the shrubbery at the side of Sarah's house. This was not easy, not at all. This had passed difficult and gone on to near impossible.

He wanted to just say it, but how did he do that?

She'd been so welcoming, so happy to see him. In that gown, she'd looked so damned beautiful, it had taken his breath away. And now, she was so open, so eager.

More time went by without a peep from either of them, and he felt his neck stiffen with tension.

Finally, he looked at her. "I guess you're dating now," popped out of his mouth, although from where, he had no idea.

She seemed surprised, then smiled. "If you can call that a date."

"Is he...someone steady?"

"Nope. This was our very first time out, and a big mistake. David's very nice—until he drinks. I had no idea."

"How long have you known him?" Tim heard the barely-masked jealousy in his voice and cursed himself silently.

"What is this, the third degree?" Sarah had heard it, too; she had that slightly smug look on her face that women got when they knew a man felt possessive.

He forced his shoulders to rise and fall casually, then picked at a piece of lint on his sweater. "No, just curious."

"Oh. Well, David and I met on a plane a while ago, but this is the first time I agreed to get together. Deciding to go out with him was not one of my shining moments of intuition."

"Good."

"What do you mean, 'good?'"

"I mean—" he glanced up "—I love hearing that someone else isn't doing too well with this dating thing. I've been on a few unpleasant evenings myself, lately."

"Oh." She seemed less smug now. "Were they women from my list?"

"Sure were."

"I take it you didn't care for the new list, then."

"Oh, sure." He leaned his back against the post now and faced her directly. "I liked the list just fine."

Swiveling so she was also facing him, Sarah rested on the post behind her. She brought her knees up to her chest, and wrapped her arms around her legs. She and Tim were farther apart now—both physically and emotionally—than when they had begun the conversation; he wondered if she, too, was aware of that.

"Wendy Milman seemed like a good prospect," she said. "A dedicated, kind person."

"Very kind. 'Cute as a button,' I think the expression goes." He winced. "But her voice—it's very quiet. She whispers, mostly. And she kind of sings when she's talking. You feel like she's about to break out into a chorus of 'Mary Had a Little Lamb.'"

That got a smile from her. Sarah had a great smile. "Well," she said with tolerance, "some people just have musical speaking voices."

"Yeah, but it had the strangest effect on me. All of a sudden, I wondered if, underneath all that sweetness and music, she might be a serial killer."

"Oh, Tim." She giggled now; she also had a great giggle.

"No, really. I couldn't get the image out of my head. Plus, just like another one of the women you arranged for me, she had absolutely no sense of humor. I had to repeat all my jokes, then I almost had to diagram them, so she'd know where the punch line was."

"How terrible," she said wryly. "Your jokes didn't go over. Tsk-tsk. But, in defense of myself, there was no way to know. Humor is a very personal thing. For instance, I think you're very funny, but then what do I know? I still like knock-knock jokes."

"You're making fun of me."

"No, I'm not." She wrinkled her nose, looking a hell of a lot cuter than Wendy Milman when she did. "Well, not really. Just sympathizing. So what did you and the cute-as-a-button serial killer do?"

"We went out for coffee. I was kind of hungry, so I ordered a small steak. She's been with kids too long—she cut my meat for me."

Sarah whooped her laughter then, and Tim joined her, their chuckles ringing out into the evening.

A neighbor's door slammed and somewhere in the distance a dog barked, but the night was quiet and dark, except for the streetlamps and the faint yellow glow from Sarah's porch light.

He was avoiding getting to it, Tim knew, but he loved laughing with Sarah—her sense of humor and his seemed to mesh so well.

He shook his head. "Wendy'd be great for someone, I'm sure, but not this guy."

"No. I can see that."

"And then there was tonight."

"What about tonight?"

"Bachelorette number three...or six, depending. Nora Calhoun."

Sarah snapped her fingers. "The lawyer. Great eyes, at least in her picture."

"The eyes are the largest part of her. Man, is she skinny." He held his hands up, palms facing, a distance of about three inches between them. "An ad for an eating-disorder clinic. And opinionated? She knows everything—I mean, everything. Or so she thinks. She has this unfortunate habit of arguing over every little word or thought, then summing up for the jury. I got to be the jury. I lasted two hours."

So, Sarah thought, he, too, felt unhappy with other people—women who should have been the type he claimed he was seeking. All right, then.

She allowed herself to relax just a bit, to let go of some of the wariness that had crept into her attitude. But only some. Yes, he'd been amusing her, but she sensed it was because he had something difficult to say. She wondered about the gift, and why he hadn't brought it up. Maybe she could help, without seeming pushy.

Shifting her legs so they were crossed Indian-style, she leaned in and placed her hand over his, which was resting on the wooden step between them. "Oh, Tim. All those awful women. It's terrible. Poor you."

He looked down at their two hands, the first time either of them had touched the other that night. "Yeah." She heard a slight hoarseness in his throat. "Poor me."

They sat that way for a little bit, Sarah willing Tim to look up at her, to talk to her.

She knew what she wanted now, and there was no ambivalence about her feelings. She wanted Tim. Wanted to start over, to erase all the recent discord between them. The future? It would be whatever it would be. Worrying about it defeated the purpose of enjoying the present.

The feel of his skin under her palm started her juices flowing. Maybe she should have changed into something a little more seductive, she thought with an inner smile. She wanted him to take her to bed, to make their joining what she knew it could be—slow and sensual and rich with feeling.

She wanted...

Hold on, she told herself. Why did he have to be in charge of all first moves? What was she waiting for? She would tell him. Now.

"Tim," she began. "I—"

"Wait," he interrupted her, then picked up the shopping bag at his feet and handed it to her. "Here."

"Gump's, huh? What could it be?"

Then he raised his head and met her eyes. "It's not from Gump's. That's just a bag I had in the house."

The serious, determined expression on his face again erased all the sense of well-being from the moment before. He withdrew his hand from under hers and rested it on his knee. Her pulse stuttered as panic swept over her.

She opened the bag and looked inside. On the bottom, neatly folded, were her garter belt and hose. "Oh." She felt foolish now. All that buildup—in her own mind only— for this. "Thank you," she said automatically.

"Let me tell you why I'm here," Tim said. His tone of voice was abrupt.

She tried for lightness. "Not to rescue me from David?"

A brief upturn of one side of his mouth was all she got. "That was a side effect. No, I've been thinking. This whole thing, whatever it is between us, well, it's crazy." He swept his hand through his hair, mussing it up, then distractedly combing it back down with his fingertips. "All we do is get into a hassle, every time."

She waited, not daring to breathe.

"I don't want this...chaos in my life, Sarah. Maybe that's why I've avoided getting too close to a woman— hell, to anyone. I used to be a happy person, and I want that back again. I want to enjoy myself, my work, my leisure time. I want—" He stopped.

"What do you want?" She was almost afraid to ask.

"What I want—" He swallowed, then said, "What I want is for you and me to just cut it off. Right now. No more contact, no more push-pull. I mean, we both know the attraction is there, the sex could be terrific, but, you know and I know, it's not enough."

Something happened to her at hearing these words. It was as though her mind and body went into a state of suspension. She knew her heart was racing, felt herself breathing, but she couldn't move.

*Oh, my God. Oh, my God,* she kept repeating in her head.

"That's what I wanted to say," Tim continued. "A clean break. Forget we ever met. Get over it, get on with it. I leave tonight, now, and that's it." He focused all his attention on her now. He seemed relieved, as though glad to be past an extremely difficult moment.

*No, don't leave. No, give us time. No,* she wanted to say. *No, no, no.*

But she couldn't; her muscles were paralyzed, and she felt on the edge of a precipice, about to lose her balance.

She'd felt this way before, she realized somewhere in the fog of her brain. A long time ago. She'd been seven or eight, and her overprotective parents had grudgingly allowed her to go to summer camp for the first and last time in her life.

She'd been trying to learn to dive and stood on the edge of the board for what seemed like hours, bent over, arms raised above her head, her thumbs hooked around each other. At first, the other kids encouraged her, then made fun of her. But she couldn't let her body fall into the water. She just couldn't. She remembered wishing that someone—anyone—would come over and just push her in. Then she would have been forced to do it. But no one did. It was all on her.

And she wasn't up to it. Whatever awaited her in that pool was too terrifying for her to take the chance.

That was exactly how she felt now, she realized. And she wanted, oh, how she wanted, not to be scared to jump in.

Or need to be pushed.

"Tim?" she managed to say, even though her face felt frozen.

"Yes?"

*Tell me you love me.*

She did not say it out loud. She couldn't. But she needed the word.

*Love.*

Why she placed so much importance on hearing that one small word from Tim, she didn't know, but it was important. If he said it to her, she would jump in.

But she couldn't prompt him to say it. No. Then it wouldn't count.

*Oh,* she thought in despair. She was not only a coward; she was writing the script, wasn't she, and then feeling hurt because he didn't know his lines.

Two things she always told her students were: "Do not have too many expectations of your lover," and "Do not expect them to read your mind, as it places an unfair burden on the relationship." She was guilty of both.

What should she do now? What would happen now? She still felt paralyzed, unable to speak.

"Sarah?" Tim took her hand. His was warm, hers was ice-cold. "Are you all right?"

Love. Of course, she hadn't said the word to him, had she? Did she love him?

Oh, no. Had she already allowed it to get that far? She'd told Charles she'd loved him, even though what she'd felt for him felt nothing like this sweet, sad ache. Charles had reacted with surprise, then had seemed pleased and told her he felt the same.

It was the next weekend, as a matter of fact, when she walked in on him in bed with that woman.

But Tim wasn't Charles; Sarah had to remember that.

Or was he?

He didn't like scenes, she didn't make him happy, he didn't want a relationship—most definitely, not with her.

Again, there she was on the edge of the diving platform, and again, she was unnerved by the murky waters below.

Tim leaned in toward her. She felt his warm breath on her neck. "Sarah," he whispered. "Did you hear what I said? I'm saying goodbye."

Numb, she nodded, then forced the words to come out of her mouth. "I'm sorry," she whispered back. "I guess you took me by surprise."

Sitting up straight and gathering whatever strength she could, she made herself sound self-contained and reasonable. "But you're right. We'd both be better off forgetting each other."

He pulled back and stared at her. For a moment, she thought he'd been startled by her answer, but then the laugh lines around his eyes seemed to sag with resignation. "Yeah, that's what I thought, too."

In the back of her throat, she could sense the beginnings of nervous laughter that was perilously close to tears. "Tim?" she said, trembling. "It's funny, you know."

"What is?"

"Here we are, breaking up, and we've never even been out on a date. Don't you think that's funny?"

She clamped down on her lips with her teeth, so none of the hysteria could escape.

"Yeah," he replied, rising from his sitting position and brushing off his pants. "Real funny." Gazing out toward the street, he asked, "What do you want to do about David's car?"

Still in a near trance, she too got up. "I'll take care of it. You've been terrific." Without making any more eye contact with him, she opened her door. "Thank you for everything."

She went in and closed the door behind her, before he could see her trembling as she sank down onto her living-room floor and dissolved in a flood of tears.

# 12

$\longleftarrow$

The TV show was one of those half-hour ads, featuring an aging actress who had long ago starred in a successful series and was now pitching a miracle bunion remover, complete with happy-faced testimonials from around the nation. Sarah watched, trying to ignore the knocking on her front door, but whoever it was wouldn't give up. She eased herself out of the chair, pulled the tie of her robe tighter and went over to the door. "Who is it?"

"Lois. Come on, let me in."

Grudgingly, Sarah pulled open the door, blanched at the sudden infusion of sunlight and walked back into her living room. "Why are you here?" she asked sullenly.

"Because you haven't answered your phone all week." Lois closed the door behind her.

"I'm on vacation."

"Pretty sudden vacation."

"What day is it?" Sinking back into her chair, Sarah clicked off the TV.

"Saturday."

She looked up at her friend, who wore her airline's uniform of heels, short navy skirt and gold blouse. "Did you just get in? Where were you?"

"Puyallup, Washington." Hands on hips, Lois studied her. "Hey, you look awful. You have no color. You're eyes are puffy and you have dark circles underneath."

"Gee, thanks for coming. Now I feel a lot better."

"You know what I mean." Seating herself on the edge of the couch, Lois frowned. "Come on, sweetie, you're sick. Have you seen a doctor? Do you have a fever?" She put her hand on Sarah's forehead; the motherly concern made Sarah want to cry.

In the past week, most everything had made her want to cry. Probably more than three times the sum total of all the times she'd cried in her entire life.

It had been the week from hell.

Saturday night had been Tim and his goodbye.

Monday night, she'd had to teach the dating class again. Fern had gotten a bunch of her buddies to enroll with her and the class had overflowed the room.

Tuesday morning, Sarah had criticized one of her assistants for overbooking the night before, reduced the poor girl to tears, then found herself crying right along with her, and, finally, had gathered an armful of work and headed home.

She'd been here since, crying, sleeping, moping, and watching old movies on television. She felt numb, wrung out, and exhausted.

"You're so thin," Lois said.

"Thank you."

"It was not a compliment. Come on, let's find something to eat."

Grabbing Sarah by the hand, she led her into the kitchen. She opened the refrigerator, then all the cupboards. "Practically nothing. How have you been surviving?"

"I'm not hungry."

"Well, I am." She picked up the wall phone and punched in a number. While she was waiting, she pointed to one of the cane-backed chairs that circled Sarah's kitchen table. "Sit," she ordered.

Sarah sat.

"Pete's Pizza? I want a large pizza with everything but anchovies." She gave Sarah's address. "And there's five bucks extra for your delivery person if you make it within fifteen minutes. I'm starving."

After she'd hung up, Sarah asked, "Didn't you eat on the plane?"

"Please. Airline food's better than it used to be, but that's like saying a hurricane is an improvement on a tornado. Neither one is reason to celebrate."

Sarah's half smile made Lois expel a relieved breath. "That's better. Now tell me. Did someone die?"

"Not really. Well, sort of."

"That's much clearer." With a resigned sigh, Lois filled the teakettle and placed it on the burner. Then she carried her purse over to the kitchen table and fished around in it. She brought out several small bags of nuts and two overly ripe apples. Choosing the least bruised of the two, she bit into it and sat down across from Sarah. "Help yourself. Okay, let's hear it."

Sarah stared down at the wood-grain pattern on her tabletop. "Tim and I are history."

"Excuse me?" Lois put the tip of her pinkie in one ear and made a jiggling gesture. "That old Southern cotton must be in my ears. I thought you just said you and Tim are history."

"I did."

"I wasn't aware you and Tim had been together often enough to have a history. Why have you kept this from me?"

She shrugged. "You've been traveling a lot."

"Come on."

"I honestly don't know. The whole thing was kind of strange. We never really were seeing each other, just sort of winding up in the same place at the same time, I guess. Anyway. it's over."

"Why?"

"We aren't right for each other. We have nothing in common, and we always end up arguing and hurting each other's feelings. Whatever's between us, it doesn't make either of us happy."

"Well, hey, honey, sometimes it's not a smooth ride, but that doesn't mean you turn the car down without making a couple of adjustments."

"I tried," Sarah said. "Really, I did. But it's over." She felt her eyes filling again. More tears? How could there be any left?

Lois put her hand over Sarah's and squeezed. "You're nuts. You're so crazy in love with the guy that you haven't been yourself for over a month. I know the signs, and you may be fighting the feeling for all you're worth, but you really want to lose."

Sarah shook her head adamantly. "No. You're wrong."

The kettle whistled, and Lois got up to make the tea. "Keep talking."

"Even if I did feel that way—and I'm not saying I do—he's pretty adamant about how it doesn't work for him. He told me so a week ago, told me he was cutting it off, that we were to pretend we'd never met."

"He said that?"

Sarah nodded, miserable all over again.

"What happened? Did you have a fight? Did you say something that hurt him?"

"We seem to hurt each other. I'm telling you, this is one of those itches that you really regret having scratched."

Turning, Lois cocked a fist on her hip. "So you *did* scratch it." Her mouth turned up in an I-told-you-so smile. "Yeah, I thought so. How was it? Scale of one to ten."

Lowering her eyes, Sarah shook her head. There was no way she could find humor in this, no way at all. "Don't, Lo."

"Okay, okay, just kidding." She brought two steaming cups over to the table and resumed her seat. "Have you called him?"

Sarah shook her head.

"Has he called you?"

Another shake of the head.

"I see. So, then, it's definitely over."

"Definitely."

"Hmm."

The doorbell rang and Lois took care of getting the pizza and setting it down on the kitchen table. She proceeded to eat three slices, one after the other, while worriedly watching her friend pick at one.

"Oo-ee, that was good." Lois wiped her hands on a napkin, blotted her mouth, then rose. "I'm putting the rest of this in the fridge, and I expect you to finish it."

"Yes, Mom."

Lois chuckled. "Okay, then, as long as I know you're not dying, I guess I'll get out of here. I'm heading for bed and twelve hours of sleep."

"Would you like to stay here?"

"I have to feed Killer, sorry. But you call me if you need me, hear?"

Sarah nodded. She hadn't wanted company, but now that she'd had a taste of it, was reluctant to be alone again. "Thanks, Lo," she said as she walked Lois over to the door. "I'm glad you're my friend."

"Yeah. Me, too."

They hugged, Sarah holding on a little longer than she'd planned. Then she stepped away and dug her hands into her robe pocket.

Lois stood for a moment at the door, a contemplative expression on her face. Then she shook her head and put her hand on the knob.

"What?" Sarah asked.

She hesitated, then looked at her. "Look, I wasn't going to say this, but——"

"It's all right. What?"

"Would you mind?" Lois raised a shoulder. "I mean, he's real cute and all..."

"Would I mind what?"

"I'd like to go out with him, actually," she said with an embarrassed smile. "Tim, I mean."

Sarah froze. "Oh."

"I mean, if you don't mind. You said you're sure that it's over, that there's nothing between you. I'm not asking you to call him, or anything—I can take care of that myself. KCAW, right?"

"Right."

"And I can wait awhile, if you'd like—you know, if you think the two of you might get back together. Of course, if I wait too long, someone else might grab him. You know how it is—available single men, and all."

She couldn't believe it. Lois, her best friend, being so...insensitive. But maybe this was just what she needed to snap her out of her self-pitying doldrums. Maybe Lois was helping her to get on with her life. "No, no," Sarah found herself saying. "It's okay. It's fine."

"You sure? We're friends, you and I, and I don't want anything to jeopardize——"

Temper flaring suddenly, Sarah threw her hands up. "Just call the man, for heaven's sake. Okay?"

"Okay. As long as you say so."

After nudging the door closed with her rear end, Sarah kicked off her heels as she went through the mail. It was late. There had been a staff meeting, then a celebration for one of the internees whose birthday was today. It was eleven o'clock on Wednesday night, and she was bone tired.

Absently leafing through a mail-order catalog, she sank into her chair and pressed the answering machine Playback button. A pair of shoes on page 37 caught her attention.

"Sarah?" came from the machine. "It's Lo. I hope you're feeling better. Listen, sweetie, a last-minute trip came up. Four nights—tonight through Saturday. I'll be home Sunday. Be a dear and feed Killer, will you? Oh, by the way, I went out with Tim, and we had a great time. What a dreamboat. Thanks a whole bunch for your, well, generosity, I guess. Love you."

Sarah sat there, her thumb keeping her place in the catalog.

So, they had gone out after all. Four days had passed since Lois's visit, and each day since, Sarah had fought down the urge to call her and find out if she'd actually contacted Tim. As it might have appeared that she cared too much, she'd decided to wait until—and if—Lois told her.

She just had.

Sarah's eyes narrowed. What did "We had a great time" mean? Just how much of a great time?

Before she could ponder this any further, the next caller came on.

"Sarah?"

This one made the catalog slip from her fingers and onto the floor.

"It's Tim and it's Wednesday afternoon. For the next few days, I'll be out of town at a broadcasters' convention in Las Vegas. The station will be running your new spot starting tomorrow. If you hear anything you don't like, call John Clark, the assistant manager. He'll take care of you. Okay?"

He'd delivered the message in a pleasant, impersonal manner, and there'd been no mention of his date with Lois. How gallant, how kind of him, not to rub salt into the wound. The truth was, he probably adored Lois. The two of them were perfect for each other. Lois was lots of fun.

Sarah hated Lois.

The adrenaline of rage rushed through her. Reaching for one of her heels, she threw it across the room, causing a potted plant to tumble off its pedestal table and smash into pieces. Then she scooped up the catalog and tore it into smaller and smaller bits till there was nothing left to tear.

The wild, intense emotions bubbling up to the surface were too powerful to keep her in her chair, so she sprang up and began to pace. Back and forth, back and forth in front of her fireplace. Her heartbeat sounded in her ear, a rapid *rat-tat-tat*. With an emphasis on the *rat*.

Four days. Lois would be gone for four days...and nights.

And so would Tim.

My, what a coincidence.

And so soon after having their first date. Wow, what a fast worker. Which one, Sarah didn't know, but the relationship was definitely taking off at warp speed.

Throwing, tearing and pacing wasn't enough, so she stomped into her kitchen. After rooting around in the back of her freezer, she came up with a giant chocolate bar from some months ago. Ripping off the paper, she went to work on it. Frozen solid? Who cared?

She chewed and swallowed, chewed and swallowed some more. How could she? How could Lois, her best friend, go off with the man Sarah had recently been involved with, had lost sleep over and shed enough tears over to fill a saltwater pond? How could she stab her in the back that way?

Sure, Sarah had okayed it, but did she have to take her at her word? And so quickly?

She hated Lois. But not just Lois. She didn't want to leave Tim out. Boy, did she hate him!

She chomped on the candy for a couple more seconds, then stopped, her mouth crammed full of chocolate. No, that wasn't true. She didn't hate Tim.

"I love him."

She said it out loud, although the mouthful of chocolate would have made the words impossible to understand, had anyone been listening. Grabbing the edge of the kitchen sink for balance, she swallowed the candy in one gulp, and said it again.

"I love him."

She sank onto a nearby chair and rested her elbows on the table. She loved Tim.

Yes, of course, she did.

Both of her inner voices agreed, so it was silly to deny it any longer. She loved him.

However, the knowledge did not send her into a state of euphoria. She did not hear bells or feel her heart stirring. There wasn't time.

She'd admitted it; she'd said it out loud. Now, what was she prepared to do about it?

Jump into the water, Sarah, she told herself. You can do it. It's time. Past time.

Banging her fist on the table, Sarah rose from the chair.

Action. She needed to take action. And soon, before Tim and Lois...

Oh, God. Her hand flew to her mouth.

If they hadn't already.

"Sarah Dann," she said out loud. "What have you done?

"You're about to find out," she answered, and got busy making arrangements.

She'd never moved so fast in her life. A few phone calls got the name of the hotel for the broadcasters' convention, someone else to feed Lois's cat, word left at Keep On

Learning, a plane reservation and a taxi to take her to the Oakland airport. She was packed and at the door when the cab arrived, and was in Las Vegas two and a half hours after listening to those two messages on her answering machine.

It was one-thirty in the morning, but the casino was still crowded. Moving quickly through aisles of slot machines, Sarah was surrounded by sound—the *ching-ching* of levers being pulled, shouts of encouragement at the roulette wheel, people being paged over the loudspeakers, cheers at jackpot wins, booing and wailing at misses, and coins clinking as they were spat out of machines.

Sarah barely heard any of it. She was on a mission.

She could only hope Tim and Lois were postponing hopping right into the sack. In Sarah's hope-filled version, the would-be lovers first enjoyed a leisurely meal, a stroll, several hours of gambling, even some extended foreplay—a word that made her shudder. But somehow, if Sarah got to them before the actual deed, something might be salvaged.

If not, all was lost.

All. Not only a loyal friend, but the only man—she had belatedly come to realize—she had ever loved. The man whose bed she wanted to share, whose children she wanted to conceive.

Why hadn't her head gotten the message sooner? Why had it waited till it was possibly—no, probably—too late?

*No*, she told herself. She would not give in to despair. Not yet.

The front desk wasn't allowed to release Tim's room number, but they offered to call him for her. Figuring that an in-person confrontation was the best move, she declined, then buttonholed an elderly man wearing a convention badge that read National Association of Broadcasters. She wove for him a sad story about how she knew it was late but she'd misplaced her roster for the convention, and now couldn't find the person she was supposed to be meeting. Her job was on the line. Would he mind looking up Tim Pelham and telling her his room number?

The gentleman was happy to oblige, and Sarah headed for the elevators. They were located in the new part of the hotel, which resembled a theme park. Signs boasted of fireworks, a floor show every hour on the hour, and family fun, including elephant rides for the kiddies.

It was one forty-five by the time she stood in front of room 1214. Closing her eyes, she prayed, assuring the Almighty she would never ask for anything else in her life, if only this time...

After taking a deep breath, then straightening her shoulders, Sarah knocked. A minute went by, so she knocked again. After another period of waiting, the door was opened a crack, the safety chain still on.

A woman in her late twenties appeared in the doorway. It wasn't Lois. This one was just as attractive, though— tall, with long black hair that curled past her shoulders. She wore a silk kimono, which she held closed with one hand, as though she'd thrown it on in a hurry.

The woman smiled sleepily, and shoved some hair out of her eyes. She had that look, Sarah thought, that well-loved, postcoital, contented look. "Yes?" she said to Sarah.

"I'm sorry," she apologized, wishing a hole in the floor would open up, so she could disappear. "I guess I have the wrong room."

"Who are you looking for?"

"Tim Pelham."

"Tim?" The woman smiled again. "Sure, this is his room, but he's not here. If you'd like, I can—"

"Never mind."

Without waiting for the end of the sentence, Sarah took off down the hall. Too late. She'd been too late. With her hand over her rapidly beating heart, she told herself to wait until she found someplace more private before she broke down.

"I hate elevators," she said, punching and punching the Down button. When it finally arrived, the doors opened and she stormed in. As she turned to press Lobby, she saw Tim hurrying down the hall toward her.

His hair was a mess, his shirt was undone and he was trying to zip up a pair of jeans as he ran. Sarah jammed her thumb on the Door Close button, but just as the doors were shutting, Tim slammed a forearm between them and leaped in.

While the doors smoothly closed behind him, he said, "Hello, Sarah."

For the rest of his life, Tim thought, he would remember the expression on her face as she glared at him. Fury and pain mixed together; longing, resentment, heartache. Her cheeks were flushed, and her gray green eyes managed to flash rage at the same time they filled with unshed tears.

"Go away," she ordered him.

"Imagine meeting you here," he said evenly, buttoning up his shirt.

She looked him up and down. "Why are you dressing on an elevator? Did someone interrupt something?"

"Just my sleep."

"Yeah, right."

"I have to be up at six in the morning for a breakfast meeting."

As he tore open the top snap of his jeans to tuck his shirt in, the car stopped and a middle-aged couple got on. They glanced at him, then stared. Their focus shifted to Sarah, who was too intent on her anger at him to even notice them. The man mumbled something about getting the next one, then the couple scurried out.

Tim burst out laughing, glad for the excuse. What he

wanted to do was shout for joy. Sarah was here! She was here, and it would be all right. He hoped.

In the meantime, man, was she pissed off!

After giving him a dirty look, she folded her arms tightly across her chest and ignored him pointedly the rest of the way down.

When the door opened onto the lobby, Sarah moved first, but Tim grabbed her arm. "Wait up."

She shook him off. "Leave me alone."

"Sorry. I can't. Why are you here?"

"You know why." She took off, walking briskly, so he followed.

"No, I don't."

Sarah stopped near a one-dollar slot machine and whirled around to face him. "Okay, where is she?"

"Who?"

"Lois."

"Beats me. Somewhere up in the friendly skies, I imagine."

"But you went out with her."

"Yes, I did."

"And you had a great time."

"Yes, we did. She has a great sense of humor and loves sports."

"And a great body and a cute accent."

"True. Are you finished now?"

"No." She took off again.

He watched her. She tried for head-held-high briskness. But it was fruitless; she still had a walk that would keep any man up nights. Her hips rolled and swayed ever so slightly, hinting at the interior passion of the woman. She might try to cover it up, but it couldn't be done.

She was walking away from him, she thought, but she was wrong.

He allowed himself to be led through the casino to the

poker tables, where she stopped. Standing, hands on hips, Sarah seemed utterly fascinated by one particular table of players. "I think you're lying," she said. "I think Lois is here."

"Why would she be here?"

"Because she went away for four days and so did you, and you both let me know in such a way as to make me think the worst. Which I did. And I do."

Grinning, he tunneled his fingers through his uncombed hair. "Yeah, she told me you would fall for it, and she was right."

Sarah turned and looked at him, her eyes narrowed. "Lois? Fall for what? What was she right about?"

"When she and I met—"

"Where did you meet?"

"At Sully's, my favorite bar. Your friend went to work on me right away, but it took her a while to get through to me. She said I needed to make you jealous—it was the only way to get you back. I said I knew I wanted you back, but you didn't want me back. She convinced me that you did, even said you were crazy about me."

"Did she." Sarah's hands dropped to her sides, her belligerent attitude considerably lessened.

Out of the corner of his eye, Tim noticed a few people watching them and chuckling, but he didn't care. "She convinced me I was crazy about you," he said quietly. "Although I didn't need much convincing."

Sarah's mouth opened slightly in wonder. "*Are* you crazy about me?"

"Completely and totally." He pulled her into his arms and held her close. Finally. To touch her again, to feel her melt against him. To savor her smell, to—

Sarah pushed him away. "Hold it. Who was that lady in your room?"

Closing his eyes, Tim begged for patience. "That was no lady. That was Alan Carlucci's wife."

"Huh?"

When he opened his eyes, there were more onlookers—too many for comfort. He steered Sarah away toward the gift shop area at the casino's perimeter. "The lady was Mrs. Barbara Carlucci, as of tonight. She is the former Barbara Herzl. They work at the station, and as a wedding gift, I gave them my suite and took Alan's smaller room."

"But you came running out of her room, didn't you? Zipping up your pants!"

He stopped in front of a shop window filled with glittering jewelry and sequined evening dresses. Now it was his turn to cross his arms over his chest and glare at her. "You still don't trust me, do you?"

"You haven't answered my question."

He raised his voice slightly. "I was three doors down. I asked Barbara to call me if you showed up."

"Were you sure I'd show up?"

"I was sure you wouldn't. Lois said you would, and I guess she was right. Although, at this moment, I'm not sure if that's a good thing."

Sarah looked down at her feet and made a face. "God, I hate being predictable."

"Sweetheart," he said slowly, "you are, I promise you, the least predictable person I have ever known."

For some reason, this made Sarah burst into tears. Holding her hands over her eyes, she took off down the corridor. Tim ran after her. "What is it?"

"I blew it," she said, still running. "Again. I didn't trust you, or me, or anything. I love you, damn it, and I blew it."

Catching up to her, he grabbed her shoulders. "Say it again."

"I blew it."

"No, before that." Turning her around so she was facing him, he gently pulled her hands away from her tear-streaked face. "What did you say?"

Huge, beautiful eyes the color of the ocean gazed up at him. "I said I love you, you piece of—"

Instead of letting her finish the sentence, he captured her mouth with his in a crushing, demanding, I'm-taking-over kiss.

Sarah let him take over. She had no more fight left. In no time, she was leaning against him, weak with emotion, desire curling up from her toes to her head. She adored his body, his smell, the feel of his skin, the slightly rough beard. She felt her own body softening, melting, all the hard edges gone.

"Oh, Tim," she murmured. "I'm sorry. I never used to lose my temper like that. I was so upset, so jealous, I didn't know what to do with myself."

"I love it when you get angry," he said, his breath warm on her neck. "It turns me on. In case you're wondering, I love you, too. And that's a first. I've never said it to anyone."

She leaned back and stared at him. "Really?"

"To anyone."

"No, what you said before that."

"You mean when I said I love you?" His eyes were warm, his expression tender. He pushed a lock of her hair behind her ear, then stroked a finger down her cheek. "I do. So much it hurts."

Something long battered and bruised inside her healed then, under the soothing balm of Tim's care. Sarah sighed, loudly and lavishly. "Then show me."

"I thought that's what I was doing."

She smiled for the first time in a long while. "Show me some more."

\* \* \*

Later—after they'd touched each other's skin and murmured words of endearment; after they'd feasted on each other and given pleasure with passionate tenderness; after their separate bodies had combined into one trembling, joyous, love-filled unit, which had soared to a place of such extreme physical and emotional intensity that it took them a long while to return to the present, and even longer before either could speak—Sarah lay snuggled up against Tim, her head on his chest and one leg over his thigh, while his hand curled over her shoulder, holding her close.

"I love you," she said, playing with his chest hairs.

"I love you, and it's amazing how easy it is to say it to you."

"Yes." She sighed contentedly.

"I think we should get married."

Her hand stilled. "Excuse me?"

"It's what you want, isn't it?" he asked.

"Well, but you have to want it, too." The nervous flutter in her stomach signaled that they'd left the warm afterglow of lovemaking and had entered the real world.

He squeezed her shoulder. "Hey, I just asked, didn't I? You know what? As long as we're here, in Vegas, we can do it tomorrow."

She pushed herself up on one elbow and stared at him. "Tomorrow?"

One side of his mouth quirked upward. "Hey, better catch me now. With my record, I can't guarantee I'll still want to next week."

She vaulted off the bed. "That's it—I'm out of here."

He caught her halfway to the bathroom and whirled her around so she was facing him. "Lighten up, Sarah," he said with a grin. "That was a joke."

"Yeah, I figured. But it was an awful joke."

He pulled her to him. "Oh, Sarah, Sarah—" he buried his head in her hair and she reveled in it "—I'll marry you now, I'll marry you tomorrow, next year, here or on the moon. Come back to bed.''

She smiled contentedly, arching her neck so his mouth had better access to her. She felt like Maggie the Cat—all feline softness and sensuality. "I thought you had a breakfast meeting."

"I'll reschedule it."

"It's all right. Why don't you go, and I'll be waiting for you when you get back. In your bed."

"What a plan." He loosened his hold on her, then cupped her face in his hands. Her love for him overflowed as she gazed at him. "I finally figured something out," Tim said. "There's a reason I've never found the right one, never married, never took any woman seriously."

"You were waiting for me?"

"No."

She frowned. "No?"

"I'd already found you, fifteen years ago. But the timing was bad. See? Everything that happened after that—all the women, your marriage and divorce, Charles, all of it—was because fifteen years ago, I let you get away. And now that you're here, with me, I have no intention of repeating my mistake. The timing is right this time. I'm never letting you get away, never."

Her eyes filled. "Oh, Tim."

"I'm a convert, Sarah. I want everything you want—home, kids, the works. I want a mate."

"And so do—" Her hand flew to her mouth as she remembered. "Mate. Oh, Tim, the challenge. We're supposed to go back on the radio this Monday, and present a progress report."

"Oh, yeah." His brows furrowed for a moment, then a wicked gleam came into his eyes. "Just how detailed do you think that progress report ought to be?"

"Gee, I don't know," Sarah said playfully. "Maybe we could take a few days to explore the options."

He smiled—that warm, easygoing grin of his reducing her very bones to mush. "A woman after my own heart. You're on."

\*　\*　\*　\*　\*

# Back by popular demand...

# DIANA PALMER's

## LONG, TALL TEXANS III

They're the best the Lone Star State has to offer—and
they're ready for love, even if they don't know it!
Available for the first time in one special collection,
meet HARDEN, EVAN and DONAVAN.

LONG, TALL TEXANS—the legend continues as
three more of your favorite cowboys are reunited in
this latest roundup!

Available this July wherever
Harlequin and Silhouette books are sold.

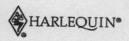 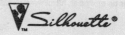

SREQ797

**They called her the**

# *Champagne Girl*

**Catherine:** Underneath the effervescent, carefree and bubbly
facade there was a depth to which few
had access.

**Matt:** The older stepbrother she inherited with her
mother's second marriage, Matt continually
complicated things. It seemed to Catherine that
she would make plans only to have Matt foul
them up.

With the perfect job waiting in New York City, only one thing
would be able to keep her on a dusty cattle ranch: something
she thought she could never have—the love of the sexiest
cowboy in the Lone Star state.

## by bestselling author

# DIANA PALMER

Available in September 1997 at your favorite retail outlet.

**MIRA** **The brightest star in women's fiction**    MDP8

## WAYS TO UNEXPECTEDLY MEET MR. RIGHT:

♡ *Go out with the sexy-sounding stranger your daughter secretly set you up with through a personal ad.*

♡ *RSVP yes to a wedding invitation—soon it might be your turn to say "I do!"*

♡ *Receive a marriage proposal by mail— from a man you've never met....*

*These are just a few of the unexpected ways that written communication leads to love in* Silhouette Yours Truly.

*Each month, look for two fast-paced, fun and flirtatious* Yours Truly *novels (with entertaining treats and sneak previews in the back pages) by some of your favorite authors—and some who are sure to become favorites.*

## YOURS TRULY™:
*Love—when you least expect it!*

YT-GEN

National Bestselling Author

# MARY LYNN BAXTER

"Ms. Baxter's writing...strikes every chord within the
female spirit."
—Sandra Brown

## LONE STAR Heat

**SHE** is Juliana Reed, a prominent broadcast journalist whose
television show is about to be syndicated. Until the murder...

**HE** is Gates O'Brien, a high-ranking member of the
Texas Rangers, determined to forget about his ex-wife. He's
onto something bad....

**Juliana and Gates** are ex-spouses, unwillingly involved in an
explosive circle of political corruption, blackmail and murder.

In order to survive, they must overcome the pain of the past...and
the very demons that drove them apart.

Available in September 1997 at your favorite retail outlet.

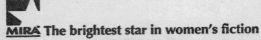

**MIRA** The brightest star in women's fiction          MMLBLSH

Look us up on-line at:http://www.romance.net